I hope this book
feels like a
gentle, if a little painful,
hug from me to you.
you're doing wonderfully,
and don't let anyone
tell you otherwise!

To all my babes with religious trauma

THE SUCCUBUS'S PRIZE

A DEAL WITH A DEMON NOVEL

KATEE ROBERT

TRINKETS & TALES LLC

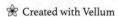

CONTENT NOTES

Tropes: Auction

Tags: a gentle cathartic hug for my babes with religious trauma, sapphic romance, demon deals, no I can't murder your entire family...but I really want to, double sided fire dildos, everyone is queer, she/they succubus, shapeshifting is sexy, did I mention the fire dildo?, sex parties, conquering shame one uncomfortable question at a time, yes I realize you having a baby would help my people but it would harm you and that makes me feral, gardening is good for the soul, JUST LET ME TAKE CARE OF YOU

CWs: religious trauma (in general, but specifically related to queerness, sex, body image, shame, the concept of sin, and the role people assigned female at birth are expected to play in being virgins and then having a bunch of children), cancer (sibling, discussed throughout), abuse (parental, religious), drugging (consensual, magical), pregnancy (discussed throughout), breeding (epilogue)

1

BELLADONNA

"Please hand me the pen. I'm ready to sign now."

The man sitting across from me is attractive in the way I've been taught devils are: dark hair that's just long enough to flop attractively across his forehead; skin so smooth I can't see pores, that probably tans wonderfully in the sun; a fit body that tempts the unwary into sin; deep-brown eyes that are almost black and seem to contain the cosmos. The only thing about him that doesn't quite mesh with his perfect image is the dismay on his handsome face.

He moves the hand holding the pen away from me. "I'm concerned that you're not taking this seriously."

If only he knew. My soul has been tainted from the moment I was born—at least to hear my parents tell it. My birth almost killed my mother, a long and bloody battle that she chooses to recount whenever I'm being particularly difficult—which means it happened regularly during my childhood and practically daily once I became a teenager who started asking questions, and now occurs basically whenever we talk. To hear my parents tell of it, that birth portended a child who would be a trial unlike any other. It's why they named me Belladonna. Deadly. Sinful. To them, my name is the same thing, and they never let me forget all the ways I've failed.

Why *not* be useful for once in my life?

I don't make a grab for the pen. It will only alarm this self-proclaimed demon, and I need this deal. *Ruth* needs this deal. "I understand the terms. I'll give you seven years, though it won't seem like that here in this realm." Multiple realms, more than heaven and hell and earth. I'm not sure I believe *that*. I barely believe in heaven and hell at all anymore. I clear my throat. "I won't be forced to do anything I don't want to do, but if I choose to have a child in your, ah, realm, then the child will stay there when I return. In exchange, you'll ensure my sister gets her cancer treatments, has acceptance to a college of her choice once she's healed —all expenses for both treatment and school paid—and has access to a trust fund after she turns twenty-five."

His sensual mouth thins. "Yes, those are the terms, but—"

"Then I would like to sign now. I'm sound of mind." More or less. I don't think being fundamentally flawed counts against me. I understand the decision I'm making; that's the only thing that matters. "Aren't you supposed to be pleased I'm making this easy on you?"

The demon—Azazel—leans back and surveys me critically. It's a look I'm used to seeing, one searching for flaws to exploit. But when he speaks again, it's not cutting and cruel. It's . . . soft and kind. "Does your family know you're doing this for them?"

"No." Of course not. They would already be on the phone, trying to schedule another exorcism. When I was a child, they had a difficult time finding a priest willing to perform one, so they switched churches. Their current pastor has all the zeal of a prophet. *He* has no problem performing exorcisms—or getting creative when they apparently don't work. I shudder at the memories threatening.

I'm not doing this for whatever purpose Azazel is about. I'm not even doing this for my parents. I'm doing it for Ruth.

Committing to this deal means I can never go home again. My mother, in particular, seems nearly supernatural when it comes to telling if I've done something God—and the family—wouldn't approve of. I don't stand a chance of hiding this. Understanding that is a strange sort of relief. I don't know where I'll go when I come back or what I'll do or how I'll survive, but maybe the constant guilt plaguing me over how I'm failing them will finally release me.

But I *will* see Ruth again, though. My sister may not share my doubt, may accidentally cut me on the edges of her faith, but she alone among my family has tried to love me. Sometimes that hurts almost more than my parents' barely concealed loathing. But she'll be alive. She'll have a chance to go to college and be exposed to the big, wide world. Maybe she'll even be able to look at me without worry in her hazel eyes.

"Belladonna..."

Good gracious, he's going to try to talk me out of this. "You aren't a very good demon, are you?" I force a laugh, the sound merry and bright and completely at odds with how tumultuous my stomach is. I've always been good at lying— except when it comes to my propensity for sin. Lying to make everyone around me more comfortable? That's child's play. Cheer puts people at ease, releases the tension in their shoulders, pulls up at the edges of their mouths. It's how I learned to stop Ruth from worrying about me, day in and day out.

Except it doesn't work with Azazel. He just blinks those deep-brown eyes like I've shocked him, and a flash of crimson shines from their depths. The crimson is too unnatural for him to be anything other than the demon he claims. "Excuse me?"

"I'm willing. I understand the cost. You have no reason to turn me down. Please hand me the contract." I do my best to appear nonthreatening and wait for him to decide. He seems to have forgotten that *he* approached *me* initially with his offer.

To hear my church tell of it, demons are waiting on every corner to tempt the unwary onto a path of sin. I had convinced myself they don't exist, and yet here one is. It's strange. I should probably be falling to my knees and calling for God to save me, but . . . this isn't some merciless beast ready to drag me to hell. He looks *stressed* at the very idea that I may take this deal.

Which honestly just reinforces my growing belief that if there's a god out there, They aren't the one worshipped by my family and church. If they were wrong about demons, surely they're wrong about God too.

This deal might all be some extravagant set-up by Pastor John, but I don't think it is. Surely Azazel would be more gleeful to have caught me in his trap, more prone to reinforcing all the ugly beliefs that have been drilled into my head all my life—would have done something to scare me back to the welcome arms of the church. Instead, he's trying to talk me out of it.

It likely says something unflattering that this demon has more morals than I do, but I'm not willing to examine this strange experience too closely.

Finally he seems to nod to himself, and he passes the contract over. "So be it. Sign here, and we'll go immediately."

The dread I keep expecting is nowhere in evidence. Understanding that is a strange sort of relief. My signature is more sprawling than usual, but it will do. Azazel still doesn't look happy as he holds out his hand and waits for me to slide mine into his. I do so without hesitation.

Just like that, the diner disappears. My stomach experiences a strange whoosh, and then we're standing in an unfamiliar room. Dizziness makes my head spin. I blink and blink again, trying to take in the massive creature holding my hand.

Where once a handsome white man stood, now there's a seven-foot-tall crimson demon. The Devil. *This* is accurate enough to the monsters of my youth that I can't stop myself from jerking my hand out of his and stumbling back. "Oh, God."

"Belladonna, breathe."

The voice is the same as Azazel's, deep and soothing enough that I can't help but obey. My brain stops buzzing long enough to register that while he looks like a demon straight out of one of Pastor John's sermons, his deep-brown eyes are the same as he waits for me to calm down. Kind. Empathetic. "Okay. Of course you look like a demon now. That makes sense."

"My glamor only works in your realm."

"Sure." I let that bounce right off me and turn to study the room. It's a bedroom larger than any I've seen in person; there's even a *sitting room* sectioned off from the giant bed that looks like something out of a fairy tale.

I can't help myself—curiosity has always been my downfall—so I walk over, wondering at how thick the rug feels beneath my worn shoes, and press my hand to the mattress. "I thought you said your name was Azazel," I whisper without looking at him. "Surely you must be Lucifer."

He snorts, sounding so like himself that my fear recedes even farther. He may look the part now, but he's hardly what I would expect of a demon—or devil. "He's a myth. I'm not."

Lucifer, a myth? My mother would go cold and scary if I dared utter such a thing. My father would rage at my disrespect and tell me how God would punish me for my lack of belief. And Ruth? She would hold my hand and tell me how worried she is about me, how she loves me but wishes I wouldn't upset our parents.

I swallow hard. "Then . . ." No, no, I just need to *think* instead of reacting. There's a reason my parents cast me out, after all. The only thing worse than someone who hasn't heard the Gospel is someone who *has* and still turns away. The very last thing my mother said to me was that I'd burn in hell. Maybe she was right.

"I'm a bargainer demon." Azazel speaks slowly and calmly. "My realm touched yours in millennia past, before an apocalyptic event thrust them apart, and even now my people can come and go. Humans have seen us and decided to conflate us with this 'hell' many of you are so terrified of." He shakes his head. "Regardless, you're not going to burn or anything similar."

My brain feels strange in my skull. Even though I've constantly been in trouble for asking questions about the faith I was raised in, and have made the decision to divorce myself from it completely, it's still shocking at times to realize how deeply the roots of belief go inside me. "Right. Of course. I'm sure that wasn't a flattering comparison. I'm sorry."

"Don't be." He waves it away. "You're not the first with

this flavor of scars to come to my realm, and I doubt you'll be the last. Regardless, the contract is signed and I will fulfill my side of things. Your sister will be taken care of." He's got his expression locked down, so I can't tell if I've insulted him or not.

The contract. I inhale slowly, then exhale just as slowly. That's why I'm here. Not for my parents, who hate me despite their creed of forgiveness and love. For Ruth, who tries to love me as best she's able. If her love hurts, well, so much in life hurts. With this choice, I've ensured her cancer treatments will be paid for, her college, her everything.

"There is clothing here for you." He nods at the wardrobe that would be at home in *Beauty and the Beast*. Honestly, I'm half-surprised it doesn't burst to life as I cross to it and pull the door open. Inside are what appear to be dozens of gowns in a full rainbow of colors. There's a vanity next to the wardrobe with small containers that must be makeup or hair products, all pristine and perfect.

I take a quick step back. "It's too much." Too much luxury. Too much color. Too many fabrics that I am *dying* to run my hands over, which is a sure sign I shouldn't do it.

"Belladonna." There it is again—a tone I can't quite define but I'm sure I should feel guilty for causing.

I take a deep breath and turn to face Azazel. "Yes?"

"You just signed away seven years of your life." He says it almost gently, but as he studies my face, something akin to understanding lands on his. He shakes his head, and his tone goes hard. "You are representing *my* household in the upcoming event, and I expect you to dress as such. The house will summon you when it's time." He turns and walks to the door, which opens before him without anyone touching it.

I'm left staring in confusion. Which is the lie? The kindness or the cruelty? I honestly have no idea.

With a mixture of reluctance, excitement, and guilt, I turn back to the wardrobe. "Well, if it's *required*, then I suppose I don't have a choice." I recognize that this reasoning is flawed and kind of sad, but twenty-five years of living under rules I had to backflip through created habits I don't know how to shake. Even the desire to shake them inspires the kind of guilt I can't quite combat.

I run my hands lovingly over the fabrics, pink and blue and green and black. I skip over the white—I'm no virginal bride, to my mother's everlasting dismay since some *worried* member of the church called her to report that they'd seen me and my boyfriend at the time having sex in his car. It doesn't matter that I thought it was love and that sex felt like a natural expression of my feelings, that he promised to marry me after we graduated high school, that he said we were already married in the eyes of God. According to my parents, I gave away the last innocence I had, and they never let me forget how damaged that now makes me. Imagine how they would rage if they knew I lust after women equally, even if I've never acted on it.

My gaze lands on a brilliant red tucked into the corner, brighter and more sensual than anything I've ever seen. My hands shake as I tug it off the hanger and hold it up to my body. Surely it's too small—my supposed gluttony is written in my soft stomach, in my wide hips, in my inability to say no to the short-lived comfort that food brings.

But it's not too small.

When I strip out of my faded clothing and pull it on, the dress doesn't pinch or pull or squeeze. It fits perfectly.

My throat threatens to close as I move to stand in front of the large mirror I've been avoiding since arriving. I . . .

look like a stranger. Someone bold and brazen and at home in her skin. The dress drapes sensually over my upper arms —leaving my shoulders and a good portion of cleavage bare —hugs my ribs and round stomach, and then falls in textured waves to the floor. I look like some kind of stylized Grecian courtesan, ready to be presented as a gift to nobility.

I fist the fabric and exhale slowly, peace settling over me. I have no choice. Oh, Azazel promised I wouldn't be forced to do anything, but he had to say that to get me to sign the contract. If I'm to be a gift, then certain things will be expected of me—a price to be paid to ensure my sister is taken care of for the rest of her life. If there's a prospective child in the mix, then that means sex. I have a choice, yes, but at the same time, there's none.

It's honestly a relief. If all choice is gone, then maybe I can be free of the voices in my head that prevent me from living life to its fullest. I've walked away from the church, but it haunts me in a way I don't know how to escape.

I'm not foolish enough to compare myself to Esther, to the biblical Ruth, or to the other women who have bargained themselves and then been held up as paragons of feminine sacrifice—if there's a lesson to be learned there, I've likely learned the wrong one.

So be it.

I've just finished pinning my hair into place and dusting some gold onto my cheeks when the door eases soundlessly open. I take a deep breath and relax my shoulders, then paste a happy smile on my face.

It's go time.

2

RUSALKA

"Rusalka."

I almost ignore Azazel's quiet call, but while dragons and krakens may get away with shitty manners, I'm not inclined to toy with the bargainer demon's temper. We have an understanding, after all—the bargainers bring humans into this realm for their own reasons, and we gain access to those humans' dreams. My people benefit from the small influx of power without having to stretch themselves to try and traverse the realms. We can't physically leave the way bargainers can, but we can travel psychically. It's just hard and takes almost as much energy as we gain from coaxing intense dreams from humans.

If our agreement means I have to kiss Azazel's boots periodically, then so be it. All for the benefit of my people. *Anything* for the benefit of my people. It's what good leaders do.

That doesn't mean I like being in the magical castle Azazel calls home. He may be a fair leader, but it's impossible to forget the wars of the past with his predecessor. *She* would have done anything to get her hands on the leaders of the other territories, to conquer the entirety of this realm.

My thoughts already have me on edge. I may trust Azazel in some regards, but I'm not a fool. If we are reluctant allies currently, that only holds so long as we find each other useful. It can change at any moment, depriving my people of their main source of sustenance. Which means I have to play nice.

None of that explains why I'm *here*. Summoned.

I turn on my hoof and wait for Azazel to catch up. Bargainer demons come in all shapes and sizes, but Azazel, king of the bargainers, is massive. His curling horns nearly scrape the ceiling, and his broad shoulders take up the hallway. He wears a wrap around his waist, leaving his dark-red chest bare. He's handsome, as bargainer demons go, but even I'm not foolish enough to toy with him that way.

He stops a respectful distance away. His predecessor would have crowded in. Caesarea always had something to prove. She was a pain in my ass, demanding much and giving scraps in return. I'm glad she's dead and gone.

I lift my brows. "Why am I here, Azazel?"

"I have a . . ." He glances over his shoulder and curses. "We're not friends."

That's the understatement of the century. "Nope."

Azazel nods. "But we *do* have a mutual understanding when it comes to humans, their needs, and what they can offer this realm. It's why I allow you access to the ones brought in by my people. You have care with them."

What is the canny bastard on about now? I school my features into polite interest—or as close as I can manage. "Yes," I say slowly. He's taking an angle, but I'm not sure what it is. My patience wanes and I sigh. "Spit it out, Azazel."

"I've already issued the details to the other leaders, but—"

"You excluded me from the invite." Shock slaps me in the face. I expect this disrespect from the other territory leaders, but I was foolish enough to assume Azazel would continue to be different. I should have known better. "What the fuck?"

"I had my reasons." He looks away, clearly uncomfortable. "As I said, we have a mutual understanding and I thought it would be better to speak of it in person."

I almost turn around and walk away, but we both know I can't afford to be excluded from any meeting involving the others. My people's safety is worth more than my pride. "I'm here. Speak."

He sighs, the sound almost silent. "I am offering a contract to every leader in this realm. A chance to have direct access to a single human for seven years. They will return to the respective territories and any children resulting in those potential unions will—"

"What?" My breath stills in my lungs. My people may have access to humans in their dreams, but the bargainers are the only ones who have physical contact with them. And the bargainer demons are jealous captors—or protective, depending on who you ask. Personally, I think it's a combination of both.

Regardless, the result is that only the bargainers have been able to procreate with humans and bolster their territory's magic. Through some quirk of evolution, when a human and a paranormal breed, the resulting child is exponentially more powerful. Here in this realm, each territory's magic is only as strong as the territory's leader's. If that leader has recent human ancestry, they—and their territory —have a decided advantage over the others in this realm.

There was a time when travel between the realms was more common, and procreation between humans and other species was too, but after the realms separated, bloodlines made more magical by humans thinned through the years. Now they're more memory for most territories than anything else. What Azazel promises will change everything. Possibly in catastrophic ways.

"Why would you do that?" I finally ask. "You have the market cornered on power right now. Why give that up?"

"The entire realm suffers because of the imbalance." He shakes his head sharply. "My predecessor—and her predecessor—tried it that way, and we've seen dozens of wars as a result. Better that everyone stands on even ground. There will be a contract. No one will force the humans to do anything they don't want to do. I'm not offering anything more than a chance at a better future."

A chance is significantly more than we've been offered before. This may be a trap; if something seems too good to be true, then it usually is. I take a deep breath. "Why not tell me the same way as the others? I thought you had more respect for my people than your predecessor."

"I do. I realize in hindsight that I mishandled this. I apologize."

An apology. That's something. I shove down my pride. "So why?"

"Because one of my candidates is . . ." He shifts almost nervously. I've never seen Azazel nervous once in our many years as leaders. He stills and meets my gaze steadily. "You have proven yourself to be a fair and considerate leader to your people. I don't believe our values are dissimilar."

I should probably do something to stop this strange reaching out he's doing; nothing good comes of other territory leaders thinking they can anticipate your moves. But I don't. Partially because I'm curious, and partially because he's right. I've worked hard, sacrificed much, and committed unsavory acts to ensure my people don't abuse their connections with dreaming humans. Historically, that wasn't something our people worried about. Now it is. And we all prosper as a result.

"I'm listening."

"You know what I'm offering and what it means to this realm, but the cost of any harm coming to the humans I've made a bargain with is devastatingly high. I'm concerned *this* human will not advocate for herself. She worries me."

I don't ask him why he made the bargain in the first place if that's true. No doubt he had his reasons. Azazel is a ruthless bastard at times, but he's got a soft heart when it comes to his humans. Whatever drove this human to make a bargain, it must have been bad enough for Azazel to override his hesitation. "Why not give her to Sol then? He's so damned careful, he's likely to spend the next seven years making polite small talk." The dragon king isn't a bad man, as such things go, but he's dreadfully boring. Which means he's safe.

"Like I said, I don't think she'll advocate for herself. Sol and the others might not realize there's a problem until it's too late and harm is done." He leans forward. "You know humans, Rusalka. More, your powers can read her desires— and lack thereof. You won't harm her or allow her to harm herself."

Normally, I'd hate that he's so sure of me, but he's not wrong. This opportunity could shake our realm to the very foundations, but I haven't fought this hard for my people to stop now. This human may be a trap waiting to be sprung. "Bram can read emotions as easily as I can."

He gives me a severe look. "Bram doesn't know what he wants."

Azazel's also not wrong about that. I shrug. "If you're so worried about her, then why don't you take her?"

"I have other priorities at the moment."

I'm mostly arguing for the sake of arguing. I won't do a single damned thing to endanger this offer. "Very well, I'll take this human and care for her. But you must know that I *will* do my best to convince her to have a child to benefit my people." The rest of the territories—Azazel excepting—don't take us seriously. If there were to be a power imbalance with my people on the wrong side? No. I won't allow it to happen.

"I know." He moves past me in a graceful step that I admire despite myself. "Follow the hallway to the end and go through the door. We'll get things started shortly." Azazel opens a door that most definitely wasn't there a moment ago and steps through.

"The bargainer castle is so damned creepy," I murmur. *Our* walls have the decency to stay where we built them, rather than change on a whim. A low rumble shakes the floor beneath my feet, and I flinch. "No insults meant." I'm not certain the castle is sentient . . . but I'm not certain it's *not*.

Either way, the rumbling stops, and I'm able to make my way down the hall to the door there. It leads into a large room with a dais on one side and several chairs and seating arrangements obviously meant for me and the other territory leaders. There's the gargoyle, Bram, with his dour expression and leathery-looking wings. Thane, the kraken leader, enters next with his equally dour expression and inset pool of what smells like salt water. And here comes Sol, the dragon leader, looking like someone just took a piss on his foot and ruined his day. But then, he always looks like that. A cheery bunch, this group is not.

Azazel appears seconds before the door opens and five human women file out. The bargainer demon truly is putting on a show, because they move to a short dais I'd missed before and step up onto it. All are dressed in luxurious gowns. Several appear terrified.

I glance at Azazel, and his gaze flicks to the woman in red. Mine, apparently. She's pretty, but all of them are; her long dark hair is gathered up around her face, and her red gown shows off smooth shoulders and the top curve of her breasts. She's also smiling as if she's having a marvelous time.

Reaching out with my magic tells another story. She's intrigued by all this, but it's almost as if the more intrigued she is, the more shame she feels. The mix coats every inch of her, thick enough that I can taste it on the back of my tongue. Familiar. How many dreams have I visited with this very combination? I've never had to deal with the person attached to the desire and shame, though, only to draw forth their deep yearnings until I'm filled to the brim with them. I know how to do *that* but not what they feel in the morning when they awake, shivering and throbbing and sick with need.

I have a feeling I'm going to discover the answer to that soon enough.

"Red," I say, barely waiting until Bram chooses his woman to claim this one as mine.

3

BELLADONNA

When the lights come up and several of the other women make shocked noises, I can only look to the demon standing near the center of the room. She must be a demon, though a different variety than Azazel, who looks like the devil I was taught to fear. I can't help the way I shake when I catch his large red body out of the corner of my eye. Azazel has been nothing but courteous with me, and yet I'm still smiling wildly to avoid cowering.

But the other? The woman—though I shouldn't assume gender. I've learned that, can do better. The *person* with the coyly melodious voice that spoke the color of my dress and claimed me as their own. They are tall, nearly as tall as Azazel, but built much leaner. They wear a gown of many colors that flares out around them when they walk, revealing legs that morph from human above the knees to that of a . . . goat's? Fur and cloven hooves. They even have a tail that whisks behind them, strangely graceful. It's oddly charming.

Above the waist, they appear human enough, with

smooth pale skin, full breasts, and short white-blond hair. I can't see their eye color at this distance, but I can tell their lips have a wicked curve, which makes things low in my stomach heat.

And there are flames licking at the edges of their shoulders and arms. At first I think they're a trick of the light, but no, they are actual flames. None of the other monsters in the room seem that concerned, but why would they be, with their tentacles and wings and scales?

What *is* this realm, which contains monsters and demons who are both so human and so decidedly *not*?

There's no opportunity to ask. I'm separated from the other humans; we're each put with our respective monster and ushered through doors that I'm nearly certain appeared with a faint shimmer while Azazel was talking.

The room my monster and I end up in looks like a perfectly mundane study, if an expensive one. Not overtly, but the signs are there in the thick carpet beneath my feet and the luxurious deep green on the walls . . . ansd the massive desk that looks like it's hundreds of years old. Or at least what I imagine a desk would look like if it was that old.

My monster sinks into one of the upholstered chairs and stretches out their . . . hooves. They watch me with undisguised interest but show no signs of speaking.

I take a deep breath and catch the faint scent of cloves. I will be here for seven years. The very least I can do is dredge up some courtesy. "I'm Belladonna. What's your name?"

"Rusalka."

The name is just as beautiful and dangerous as this monster seems to be. I clear my throat. "What—um—I mean . . ." I can do this. I don't know why my hard-won charm falters in the face of this monster's increasing amusement. I try again. "What are your pronouns?"

"Aren't you just the sweetest thing," Rusalka murmurs. "I'm not overly precious about pronouns, but 'she' works well, or 'they,' I suppose, if you'd like to use that. Gender is a bit fluid for most of my people."

She. They. Two pronouns. Okay. That bends my mind a little, but I'll be damned before I ask her to explain. I'll figure it out. I do my best to banish my mother's derision to the recesses of my mind. It doesn't matter what my mother thinks of *pronouns*. It matters what *I* do.

My smile feels brittle at the edges, shaky. "Your people?"

Something softens in her eyes, which I can now see are a deep amber that almost seems orange, though surely that's impossible. People don't have *orange* eyes. Then again, people don't have cloven hooves and tails and fire that dances along their short blond hair either. Strange that the room feels just as pleasantly chilly as it did when we walked in.

Rusalka slowly crosses one leg over the other. "My people are the incubi and succubi."

Incubi. Succubi.

These terms I know. Pastor John used to rant about the sins of the flesh, sins that somehow also extended to the mind, and he claimed a good person could be ensnared by the wiles and magic of a succubus. I'm pretty sure he meant women who aren't afraid to have sex out of marriage, since he was always fond of exaggerated metaphors. Though if I pointed out as much to my mother, I was destined for . . .

I shudder. No. Damn it, *no*. I owe nothing to the parents I've been disappointing since birth. No marriage to a good God-fearing man who will lead the family, will protect, will . . . I shudder again.

"Belladonna." Rusalka leans forward, drawing me out of the spiral threatening to suck me under. "Breathe, love. Just breathe. Slowly." Her voice is soft, but there's no ignoring the command in it.

If I were better at obeying commands, I wouldn't be in this position to begin with, and yet I find myself inhaling, matching the cadence of my breathing with hers. Again and again, until surely she must be tired of coaching me through something instinctive to every other human in existence.

But Rusalka never takes her strange orange eyes from mine, never lets impatience enter her honeyed tones as she keeps speaking until I've calmed down.

I lick my lips. "Thank you."

"You don't have to sign the contract, love. I'll not force you, and Azazel would find some sword to fall on before he pressured you into this."

So he's told me. Several times. I don't know what to do in the face of her unexpected kindness. The hell I was always threatened with is fiery and unfeeling and empty of any comforts. "I know."

She waits, but I don't accept her offer of a graceful exit. Rusalka sits back. "I understand why the canny old bastard came to me."

I let their words slide over me. I don't know what they're talking about, but I don't suppose I need to know. "I'll adjust. This is all new to me. I didn't expect. . . you."

Rusalka laughs, and the sound wraps around me like a warm embrace. "Few do."

I don't know what she would have said next, because the door opens and Azazel steps in. He glances from me to the monster beside me, and though it's hard to tell on his equally monstrous face, he looks concerned. "Is there a problem?"

Rusalka doesn't answer, leaving me to speak. "No." I shake my head sharply. "Everything is fine. I'm ready to sign the secondary contract." A contract that will bind me to *Rusalka* for the duration of my time here. Azazel explained it to me before I signed the first one—how he wouldn't be the one I'd be dealing with for the duration of my service. I think he was hoping it would make me change my mind, but what does it matter who I serve?

"Belladonna," he starts. "At least *read* the second contract before you do."

"It doesn't matter." I don't mean to say it. I'm not supposed to say things like that, to make people uncomfortable by revealing the deep well of hopelessness that resides inside me. A God-shaped hole, though the more I tried to offer myself to Him, the wider the hole became. Until I stopped trying entirely. According to my parents, I just needed to believe harder, to stop doubting, and that would fix everything. Even Ruth wanted that for me. Faith comes so effortlessly to her. She never really understood why I fought against it. If she loved me despite my so-called flaws, she could never quite forget the flaws exist.

I am a horrible disappointment of a daughter, but I'll be damned twice over before I balk at what needs to be done now. My parents are content to pray over my sister until God heals her cancer. They'd rather she die than lack the faith to see herself well again, as if her cancer is punishment for something she's done, rather than a terrible thing that happened to a good person because the world is random in its cruelty the same way it's random in its kindness.

Well, fuck that. My sister will get the treatment she needs, and she'll *live*.

I shove to my feet and grab the pen lying on the desk, ignoring Azazel's sharp protest, then scrawl my name on one of the lines for a signature. I spin to face him. "There. It's done. Please stop trying to talk me out of this."

He looks like I picked up a gun and shot him: in shock and something almost like pain. He turns to Rusalka. "I've changed—"

"The human has made her choice." Rusalka still has that glorious, terrible, and soft amusement in her rich tones. She reaches one long arm over and picks up the pen to sign before Azazel can protest further. "Don't worry, darling. I'll take good care of her."

I expect that to rile him further, but some of the tension in his broad shoulders eases. He pinches the bridge of his nose. "So be it. Understand that if you misjudge this and harm her, your kingdom is forfeit."

"Consider me cowed and obedient." Rusalka sounds anything but. They rise slowly to their impressive height and hold out a hand, which I belatedly realize shifts to black at their fingers . . . their *claws*. "Come along, Belladonna. It's time to go home."

Home.

There might have been a time when the concept of home was as warm and comforting as the movies make it seem, but I can't remember experiencing that for myself.

It doesn't matter. The only peace I find is in the inevitability of sin, of the moment when I know I shouldn't do a thing but do it anyways, pulled forward by an impulse I've never learned to fight. Not for all the prayer and punishment and extreme interventions. Rejecting the church's teachings hasn't cured me of that dangerous impulsiveness. If anything, sometimes I swear it's made things worse.

What's one more mistake? At least someone actually benefits from it this time. I slip my hand into Rusalka's and allow her to pull me to my feet. "I'm ready to go . . . home."

4

RUSALKA

I understand now. This human will require careful handling. I hadn't really thought Azazel was over-stating things, but it was difficult to fully credit his concern before meeting Belladonna.

She's magnificent, even while fighting herself. How fiercely would Belladonna shine if not for the shame clinging to her, weighing her down like a widow's shroud? I have a feeling it would be fierce indeed. And I have every intention of finding out.

The magic of the bargainer demon's castle provides a quick exit back to my territory. It's one of those strange quirks that are all but impossible to ward against, one that caused my territory no end of grief when we were at war so long ago. It may be difficult to march an army through a single door, but an assassin? My predecessors' records are immaculate; as a result, Azazel never postures to remind me of what he's capable of. He knows I will never forget.

Even so, it's a relief to step through the door and back into the pleasant warmth I'm so used to without many days' journey. I keep Belladonna's hand clasped in mine as I turn to shut the door and throw the bar across it.

She watches with wide eyes. "Is that really enough to stop magic?"

"No." I shrug. "But it makes everyone feel better, and sometimes that's the most important thing." I can see her lack of understanding in the small line that appears between her brows. "I'll show you to your rooms, and then I'll hunt down some food to settle your nerves."

I note the way she almost flinches but muscles through her instinctive response. This one is a fighter. I approve.

"Settle my nerves," she echoes. She smiles, the expression bright and sunny—and a complete lie. "That sounds . . . nice."

I keep moving, tugging her along with me. My Insomnior Court will show up before too long, looking for an update and to assure themselves that I'm fine after the meeting with Azazel. Normally I would seek them out immediately to discuss this turn of events, but I suspect Belladonna is reaching the end of her ability to process new things.

I lead her to the consort's rooms. They've stood empty since I took my title. I haven't had time to indulge in a proper consort; ruling this territory takes up too much time and energy. All my romantic encounters are restricted to sex only, and I avoid partners who look at me with stars in their eyes. Better that everyone involved has the same expectations. I've only misjudged a few times, and the pain it's caused has ensured I am particularly careful now.

It worries my court. They've been pressuring me for years now to settle down with a consort. I don't think my taking a human as one is what they meant, but they won't be able to argue the end result.

"Stay here for a moment. I'll be right back." I take the time to ensure she sits before she falls down, and then I whisk out of the room.

Inna appears before I take two steps, shadows clinging to their features, nearly obscuring their deep-crimson eyes. Like most incubi, they're built slighter than I am, their head barely coming up to my shoulder. Their skin is moon pale and their hair nearly the same crimson as their eyes. Our forms are similar enough—humanoid but with cloven hooves and a tufted tail—but incubi magic leans toward shadows while succubi favor fire.

"That was a quick meeting."

"You have no idea." I keep moving, allowing them to fall into step next to me. "Two hours, and then I need the rest of the Insomnior Court together in the usual spot. You can ask your questions then."

Surprise makes their shadows flare. "Something happened."

"Yes." The kitchens are on the floor below the rooms. The leader's seat is significantly smaller here than in the other territories. We have no need for castles, either above or below the waves, no need to style ourselves as monarchs. This manor house has rooms enough for half a dozen people and is situated right on the main square of our largest town. We succubi and incubi are social creatures and significantly more informal than those in the other territories. Everyone else wants to be a little king, to wield what power they have over those within their control. Not so, here.

It's been a point of contention in the past. The other territories patronize us for the way we do things, for how communal we are, for our informal power structures. They see us as weak, which usually means that when conflict comes, it comes to us first. It's been a long time since we've fought with weapons, but trade is just another kind of war. I've worked for decades, have sacrificed time and energy and kindness, to ensure that my people want for nothing.

With the prize Azazel just offered us all, we could have a prolonged peace . . . or another war on the horizon. Either way, I have to prepare.

Inna clears their throat. "The house feels . . . different."

Because Belladonna is here. It won't take long for the entire town to know we have a human in our midst and come sniffing around. I don't hold their curiosity against them, but I need to get her settled in properly before we brave that experience. "I'll explain when everyone is gathered. Go."

For a moment, it seems like they might argue, but finally they nod. "Consider it done."

We're in that sweet spot after lunch but before dinner preparation, so I'm able to slip into the kitchen without encountering Jitka. She's a brilliant chef and capable of great edible masterpieces but so fiercely territorial that even I hesitate to cross her. Unfortunately, what Jitka considers "crossing" her includes a number of otherwise minor offenses—like stealing apples from the bowl obviously meant for something later.

But my human needs to eat, so I resign myself to dodging a wooden spoon later when Jitka realizes my trespass.

I hurry back upstairs to find Belladonna exactly where I left her. She hasn't even roused herself to snoop. Worrisome. I cross to perch next to her on the edge of the bed and press an apple into her hand. "I'm sure you have questions. I can answer them now, or wait until you're more settled."

"Why do you need a baby?"

I blink. Well then, I suppose we'll start there. "The magic of each territory is directly linked to the person who leads it. In other territories, that leadership is passed down along bloodlines, but we do things differently here. The person with the strongest magic and the backing of the people leads. They can also be removed at any time if they abuse their power." This precaution ensures we don't end up with some power-hungry monarch like some of the other territories have seen in the past. "Through a quirk of biology, humans are great amplifiers of magic when they breed with paranormal people. Any child you have with one of our own will be easily twice as powerful as I am, and the whole of the territory will benefit as a result."

She stares into my eyes, and I taste her despair on my tongue. It's a strange response to my words. Belladonna nods before I can press her on it. "I see. So it's a small sacrifice to help a lot of people."

"A child is not a *sacrifice*." I don't mean for my voice to go sharp, but I don't trust the direction of her thoughts. "If someone chooses to have a child, then that child is a gift and a blessing."

"All children are gifts and blessings." She says it by rote, as if reciting some law.

My distrust grows. I narrow my eyes. "Back in the human realm, you worshipped that great sadist of a god, didn't you?"

That gets a response. She jerks back. "You can't *say* things like that." Then she shakes her head hard. "Sorry, that was rude. But describing Him like that . . ." She swallows visibly. "I am no longer associated with that church, but sometimes I react the way I was raised to, instead of how I believe now."

It's as much a confirmation as the shame oozing from

her pores. I have to look away, have to take a moment to lock myself down. A good leader doesn't let their emotions get the best of them, especially when being careless may hurt one of their people. By virtue of the contract, Belladonna is one of mine now. "What were the terms of your deal with Azazel?"

"Seven years of service in exchange for money for my sister, designated for treatment, college, and a trust fund." She drags in a shuddering breath. "She's sick, and I'm afraid she'll die without treatment. My parents don't have money for it, and now they have no excuse *not* to get her treatment. Azazel will make sure it happens."

There's something there, just beneath her words—a thread of anger that thrums through my bones. Curiosity almost makes me reckless, but I have seven years. I don't need every answer this woman has to give in a single hour. "Tomorrow, I'll give you a proper tour of the manor and the town, but for now, just know that you're safe."

"Safe." She gives a sad little laugh. "I suppose I am." Belladonna takes a deep breath and rises. Before I register what she's about, she pulls at her dress, sending it cascading to the floor and leaving her gloriously naked.

I am who I am. I can't help but visually trace the curve of her hips, her soft belly, her heavy breasts, each topped with perfect berry nipples. The flush beneath her skin increases with each beat that passes, spreading from her cheeks down her neck and over her chest. Lust, tentative and sweet, layers the air between us.

I clear my throat. "What are you doing?"

"Honoring the terms of my contract." The shake in her voice makes its way through her body, terror washing away that hint of lust.

Terror.

A little fear can spice up bedroom games, but this is something else. I drag my attention to her face and keep it there. "You don't want to."

"I do." Her desires are all tangled up with shame and fear and something infinitely more complicated. I can't get a proper read on her, but even if she were fully willing, things are done a certain way. This is . . . crass.

I rise, noting the way she flinches. "No, you don't." I turn away, then move to the wardrobe near the bathroom door and rifle through it until I come up with a thick robe. I retrace my steps and drape it carefully around her shoulders. She's still trembling, but as she inhales, her shivers ease.

I wait for her to look up at me before I speak. "But when you *do* want to, Belladonna?" I lean down and brush a kiss against her temple. "Well, then we'll see what's beneath all that shame you carry."

There's nothing to do but leave. She has my nerves strung too tightly. I didn't expect this, as someone who has dealt with humans more than most people in this realm. The other territory leaders would have boggled this. Sol is too intent on an heir, Thane is too cold and out of touch for anything resembling a relationship, and Bram has more baggage than Belladonna. Azazel was right to give her to me.

Still, it doesn't sit well with me.

I intended to seduce my new human to the fullest extent of my considerable abilities. Apparently I need to take a subtler approach. Being delicate hardly outside my skill set, but it's not my preferred way of moving through the world.

This is going to be . . . interesting.

5

BELLADONNA

I don't expect sleep, but it takes me in a stealthy wave, sucking me under and sending me to blessed oblivion. The dream forms around me slowly, so slowly that I barely register it until I'm sitting on a throne. The chair warm against my back and tall enough that my toes barely brush the floor. The moment I notice the floor, it's as if a veil is pulled from the scene before me.

There's a woman, dark-haired and wearing a dress held together by two tiny straps over her shoulders. She's dancing with a partner I can't quite define, their edges slipping away from me every time I try to focus on them. I'm not a dancer —music not of the church was strictly forbidden when I was growing up, a temptation designed to draw good God-fearing Christians from their path. I still haven't quite managed to stop feeling guilty when I listen to the radio, but I'm working on it. This music has no words, though. It's deep and throbbing, seeming to take up residence in my chest and . . . lower.

The woman's partner spins her, moving seamlessly from some kind of formal dance to something closer, designed to match the thrumming beat. Their hands stroke down her back, grip her hips, and pull her close. Close enough that I have to cross my legs and fight not to squirm. All that separates the two of them is clothing.

And then, in the logic of dreams, all their clothing disappears. I'm watching them closely, yet I don't register it happening. One moment they're dressed, and the next they're both naked.

They're . . . beautiful.

"I approve."

I jolt so hard, I would have fallen out of my throne if not for the way my body seems anchored to it. Next to me, where there was only emptiness, now sits an identical throne. Its occupant sits haphazardly, one long leg dangling over the chair's arm, their chin propped on a fist.

"Rusalka," I breathe. She looks different, her skin almost glowing, light moving within like a live fire. It makes me want to run my fingers over the shifting flames to see if they're warm. To have an excuse to touch her. I shake my head sharply. "You're not here."

"I think you'll find that I am."

"But . . . how?"

"Succubus, darling." She's not looking at me, her attention instead on the couple with their questing hands. One of them moans, and I can't help shivering in response to the need in that single sound. Rusalka smiles, a slow curling thing that makes her lips look particularly kissable. "Dreams are our purview. We can't travel to the human realm the same way the bargainer demons can, but my people have been visiting human dreams for millennia."

That should scare me. I think it does. Maybe. "So you're the one who's been putting *those* dreams in my head my whole life?" Not my whole life, really, but ever since I hit a certain age, I'd wake up some nights too warm and restless and *throbbing*. I thought it was a manifestation of all the sin I tried so hard to avoid during my waking hours. But if it wasn't *me* . . .

Except Rusalka is shaking her head. "No, love. We can manipulate the dreams a little, but the source is you. It's what draws us to you in the first place. Beyond that, we leave evidence behind in the way of a particular energy signature." She inhales deeply. "You've never been touched by one of ours."

I want to call her a liar, but isn't she telling me what I already know? I study her because it's easier than looking at the scene developing, the dancers sinking gracefully to the floor that's now a bed. Rusalka seems so at ease in her skin that envy sprouts its green tendrils inside me. What must it be like to experience that confidence, that comfort?

"You could find out, you know."

I shudder. "You can read minds?"

"I can read desire. With you, it's practically the same thing." She grins, revealing tiny fangs that almost look like a vampire's. "You are a burning pyre of desire, Belladonna. It's a tragedy that you are so resistant to taking what you want."

As if it's that easy, even when I *want* to take something. I drag in a breath. "I've been told all my life that it's a flaw, a sin, to want the things I do." To want the *people* I do.

"A lot of people say that. I don't care what they think." Rusalka's smile widens, but her orange eyes glow sympathetically in a way that makes me think she's not judging me. "What do *you* think?"

Even Ruth couldn't quite mask her feelings when I finally confessed that I find women as attractive—if not more so—than men. She told me that she loves me despite my sin, her expression so earnest, as if she wasn't driving a dagger into the very heart of me. That was the moment I walked away from the church entirely, the moment when the rift between my sister and me became something I didn't know how to cross. I still love her, but it hurts. It's never stopped hurting.

"How can love be a sin?" I whisper, the words rotting in the very heart of me. I asked my father that once, and it was the only time he raised his hand to me. I swallow hard and say the words again: "How can loving someone be a sin? Why does God care what I do in my bed?"

"I think you know the answer to that, love."

I hate her a little in that moment. Not for anything she's said, but for the confidence that comes from her in waves. This person has never experienced the doubt I can't seem to shake no matter how hard I try. I clear my throat. "It doesn't matter."

"I think it might." They shrug, not pressing the issue. "What do you want, Belladonna? Not your god, not your family—*you*."

"I don't know."

Rusalka chuckles, the sound an invitation I don't know how to accept. "You may not be willing to admit it, but your desire is written across every bit of you. Would you like to see?" They don't wait for a response, waving a hand leisurely in the direction of the couple.

Even as I tell myself not to, I follow the movement . . . to find the couple has shifted. No longer safely faceless, they are intimately familiar. Or at least one of them is. It's *me*, back in the bed, Rusalka hovering over me, smiling that slow smile that's an invitation to do unspeakable things.

I whip my head around to find her still sitting in the throne next to me. "What? How?"

"It was there all along, love." They sound satisfied

and . . . intrigued? Their orange eyes flare brighter as if they're gaining energy from this. "You're all raw need. Would you like me to show you the possibilities?"

No. It's bad enough that our doppelgängers are laid out, my leg wrapped around her slender hip, my fingers digging into her short blond hair. What more could she possibly offer? I lick my lips, curiosity blooming inside me. Even before I all but sold my soul to a demon, I was flawed and imperfect in a way that I stopped believing God could fix. There's no amount of faith that can change who I am at my core.

But . . .

My skin heats unpleasantly. "I can't. I shouldn't."

"Ah." I expect Rusalka to berate me, but she just hums a little under her breath, her gorgeous face contemplative. Finally, she says, "My people have many gifts, and one of them is to raise the desire in the humans whose dreams we visit. It's how we feed."

" . . . Oh." A shot of pure fear goes through me, quickly followed by desire, and then I'm doused in shame because I shouldn't be even considering taking them up on their offer. Except I am, aren't I? And that's what set me apart from my family and community before I left: knowing I shouldn't and doing it anyways. "Do it."

"Belladonna." She says my name on a sigh. "Ask me again when you wake up. I'll give you everything you want, and more. For now, enjoy the show."

I turn to ask her what she means, but she's gone, throne and succubus disappeared as if they never were. I frown, but a moan brings my attention back to the couple. They're no longer simply kissing. Rusalka's double has pressed mine down and is kissing a descent to the apex of her—my— thighs. If I concentrate, I can almost feel the brush of her lips against my heated skin. I want to blame the real succubus for this, but I know better. My dreams have always been like this, at least in sensation if not in vision.

And then Rusalka drags their tongue up my double's center. I shouldn't be able to see it so clearly, the way their tongue parts my folds and delves between them, but it's clear in the unknowable way dreams can be.

I cross my thighs and squeeze them together, but I can't begin to say if I'm trying to banish the growing heaviness of my body . . . or chase it to completion. It doesn't seem to matter.

Her tongue pushes inside my double's pussy even as she holds her quivering thighs wide, and I swear I can feel the slick sensation between *my* thighs. It makes me jump, but there's nowhere to go. Even as I command my body to rise and run, my limbs go heavy and unresponsive—except for where I grip the arms of the throne, my knuckles white.

Relief washes over me in a dizzy wave. I can't stop this. I've tried to resist it. I tried to do the *right* thing, and that door is closed to me. The only thing left to do is endure, experience this to its fullest. I close my eyes and lean my head back, letting my legs uncross and slide open. There's no other choice, is there?

This time, I don't jump when a faint moan reaches me. Or when strong hands gently urge my thighs wider. I'm certain I had clothes on just a moment ago, but they've disappeared just like my double's did earlier.

Breath ghosts over my most private flesh, and I bite my lip bloody, not certain whether I'm holding in a protest or a plea for more. It doesn't matter. The first slow drag of a tongue over me steals what words I might have summoned.

A teasing lick. An exploratory caress. It feels so wrong to be doing this, which only makes my desire spike hotter. I squeeze my eyes shut tighter. I won't look. It's not happening if I don't look. Or maybe because it's a dream. Or . . .

The attempts to reason through this leave me as they find my clit. I know that little nub of nerves intimately, courtesy of my own explorations in the darkest part of the night, but I've never had someone else touch me there. Certainly not Jacob the single time we had sex. Not with his hands and not with his *mouth*.

Rusalka—because who else could this be?—rubs the flat of their tongue over my clit, a gentle tease that makes my head fall back farther and my body go both limp and tight at the same time. Again and again, building my desire higher and tighter and . . .

"Oh my God!"

I sit up in bed, my body tangled in the sheets, my core pulsing with a fading need as my orgasm recedes. I press my hands to my scorched cheeks, my breath coming in ragged inhales. I've dreamed erotically in the past, but never on that level. Never with that detail. And never with a partner who did *that* to me.

Even as that ugly little voice in the back of my mind tells me not to, I lie back down onto the soft mattress and ease my hand between my thighs. No surprise that I'm heated and wet. Again, I ignore the voice demanding I stop, and I slide my middle finger between my folds, following the phantom path Rusalka's tongue took in my dreams. It doesn't feel the same, not really, but the imagination is a wonderful and terrifying thing, and I can almost—almost—reclaim the sensation.

Desire winds me tighter and tighter, and when I crest, it's with Rusalka's name glowing in my mind.

6

RUSALKA

"What do you mean, no one touches her?"

I bite back a sigh of irritation and turn to Zhenya. Ze is practically bouncing on zir toes, zir mass of dark curls following the movement a beat later. Zir shadows contract and expand with each bounce, creating a dizzying visual. Zhenya is tall for an incubus, nearly as tall as I am, and zir skin is medium brown in some places and pure white in others, forming a gorgeous pattern. Ze is filled with enough energy to outlast anyone I know. It's a boon in so many ways, but right now I don't have the patience for it.

The meeting with the Insomnior Court yesterday was mostly to bring them up to speed. They needed to understand the gift—and risk—Belladonna represents. The potential ramifications are something we'll circle for some time, but I was too focused on getting Belladonna settled, knowing that further answers would come when she slept . . . Well, they came, didn't they? She's a powder keg and must be handled gently.

Which means another conversation about boundaries.

"I mean exactly what I said. Let her watch. Don't touch her. Not yet."

Belladonna is curious, but the damned shame blocks everything. I'm not so arrogant as to think I can unravel a lifetime of conditioning in a few days. Walking through dreams is easier when there's only a single night of a human's dreams to engage with. I don't have to worry about what comes with the sunrise.

"But—"

"Rushing her risks harming her, which harms our people."

"Rusalka is right." Danik lounges on the couch, weaving fire between his claws. He looks well rested, his dark-brown skin gleaming in the flickering light. "Not just because the cost of harm is so high. She's the first human to set foot in our territory in longer than anyone can remember. It would be shortsighted to fumble this opportunity."

I manage a smile in response, but it feels distracted. Surely Belladonna is awake by now. Is she even now lying in bed, awash with cloying guilt and simmering need? Her dream surprised me. I should have kept my distance and allowed her to rest without interference, but her lust drew me in despite myself. I wanted to know what gave her such a delicious thrill. Imagine my shock when it was *us*, an image of me and Belladonna tangled intimately.

I didn't have to manipulate a single thing, and the sheer need she exhibited gave me a surge of power that is still leaving me restless, hours later.

My little human is curious and lustful, and I want to get to her before she has a chance to retreat behind that wall of shame. Before I can give myself several very solid reasons not to move, I'm on my feet. "I'll have her ready for the tour in a few hours. Make sure everything is ready."

Danik laughs softly under his breath. "Everything will be perfect, Rusalka. Have no doubts about it."

"I don't." I sweep out of the room, catch myself rushing, and check my stride. Even forcibly slowing myself down, I reach Belladonna's room in short order. It's tempting to walk in and surprise her, but that would cross a line. To even consider it at all rocks me back on my heels. I don't misstep, not when the consequences are so damnably high. I haven't forgotten to consider the risk to my people in any given situation in longer than I can remember, and the fact that I almost do in this moment worries me.

I take a breath and knock. The door opens so suddenly, she must have been standing in front of it. Gods help me, but I drink in the sight of her. Belladonna is deliciously rumpled, her dark hair tangled and wavy from sleep, her loose dress slightly askew, one strap slipping off her shoulder. I lick my lips before I can stop myself. "Good morning."

"Rusalka." Her voice squeaks in the middle of my name. "I, uh, hi. Hello. Good morning."

All the tension bleeds out of me after a few seconds in her presence. She's so nervous, it's impossible for me to be nervous too. I smile. "I thought you might want something to eat. Then we'll take a tour of the house. If you're not dead on your feet at that point, we can walk the town square. My people are curious about you."

Her eyes—a gorgeous deep brown—go wide. "I know the purpose I'll serve here. Surely everyone doesn't need to meet me. They'll just—" She stops herself, straightens, and clears her throat. "A tour would be lovely."

I wait for her to change and pull on shoes before I offer her my arm. I chew on her words—and what she didn't say. Part of me threatens to bristle at the idea that she might find my people lesser. Though it's nothing more than I'm used to.

Every territory in this realm is certain that they're miles better than the others, and they're *all* sure they're superior to the incubi and succubi. It stands to reason that humans think they're better than us all.

Except . . . superiority isn't the feeling I get when Belladonna lightly presses her fingertips to my arm as if ready to jump away at any moment.

I reach out to brush my magic against her and nearly flinch. Shame coats my tongue and throat, souring the breakfast I ate earlier. I shake my head sharply, trying to clear it. She doesn't think my people are beneath her. She's worried that they won't approve of *her*.

That should reassure me. Her thinking she has something to prove will make her easier to manipulate, or at least more likely to keep her word and have a child—or several—that will benefit my entire territory. I've lied, cheated, and played games that still turn my stomach in order to protect my people. Allowing one human to go through with something she agreed to when she signed the contract shouldn't count as harm. Not even Azazel could argue that.

Even though we'd both know better.

I turn abruptly down the next hallway. "Change of plans."

"Change of—" She trips over her feet, and I have to catch her elbow to keep her from falling. Belladonna shoves her hair out of her face. "Rusalka, slow down please."

I check my stride, but only barely. I don't understand the anger bubbling up inside me. I don't know this woman. I have no right to feel so protective of someone I just met. "You are a *gift*." How can she be anything else? By her own admission, she willingly gave seven years—and potentially a child—to save her sister. That kind of selflessness is rarer than lightning strikes. Even thinking about it puts a bad taste in my mouth. It's abhorrent.

"What?"

We push through the main doors and out into the cool morning air. This isn't how I planned to do things. I wanted to ease her into a very carefully curated experience of my home. To ensure she wasn't afraid and had time to adjust. To show her that my people are worth fighting for.

Instead, we stand in the main square, garnering attention from passersby, their eyes wide and curious as they take us in. The house takes up one side of the square, and the other three sides are filled with small shops. We slept late, so most of them are open, filled with people going about their business. It's nearly lunchtime and children run about in small packs, enjoying the afternoon break. Several of them wave as they sprint past, intent on their games.

"*Rusalka.*" Belladonna digs in her heels, nearly towing me to a stop. "*Rusalka*, I'm not ready."

This might be a mistake, to rush things instead of playing them strategically, but I need her to understand. If she could just *see* what I've worked so hard to protect, then maybe she would understand that there's no shame in this, no matter what her sadist of a god says. People moving about freely, without fear, interacting with *love*. We are not immune to the petty fights and bullshit that everyone experiences if they live long enough, but community is at the center of everything.

I don't have a chance to come up with the words to explain myself or change my mind about bringing her out here. People flock to us. Some of them are only vaguely familiar, having traveled in from the outskirts for market day, but others I've known most of my life. Incubi and succubi, young and old and every age in between. They don't rush, but they approach all the same, murmuring to one another in amazement as they take in the woman at my side.

Belladonna cringes closer to me, cowering behind me, and I plant my feet, giving her the solidness she obviously wants. "It's okay," I murmur, my frustration already blown out, replaced by an emotion I don't have a name for. "You're safe."

"They're *staring* at me," she whispers.

A small succubus steps forward timidly, their head ducked and long red hair braided away from their pretty face. They reach forward suddenly and clasp Belladonna's free hand in both of theirs. *"Thank you."* They duck away before she can come up with a response, but her surprise is clear and grows as my people welcome her, thank her, lavish her with praise for coming here.

A small child comes up, a blush darkening their light-brown cheeks, and passes her a rumpled bouquet of flowers. "Thank you, lady."

A grandfather cups her face and smiles, his eyes practically disappearing in his deep wrinkles. "We appreciate your service more than we can say."

A pregnant person presses a hand to their round stomach, tears in their crimson eyes. "You do us a kindness beyond measure."

Thank you and *thank you* and *thank you* again. All the while Belladonna stands perfectly still, her lips parted in shock, her eyes wide, her lip fingers barely holding the flowers. She doesn't manage a response, but no one expects a response. They're just so damned happy she's here.

I knew word would spread fast, just like I knew what the response would be. Azazel has played his cards well, though I still don't fully trust his aims. Even so, it's hard to fault him when we stand to gain so much. Peace in this realm has been uneasy since the last conflict. What better way to ensure we all keep our attention within our own borders than to give us a prize beyond measure, one to be protected and cherished and pampered.

When the crowd finally thins, Belladonna turns to me. Her eyes shine and her lower lip quivers. "Is this a trick? Did you arrange this?"

"No." It's the truth. "You being here benefits every single person in the territory. They recognize it and they appreciate it beyond measure."

Some of her shock fades away, a weary understanding taking residence. "But only if I have a baby and you make that baby the leader."

I don't mean to reach out and stroke my fingers through her long dark hair, but I can't quite help myself. She still doesn't understand. I take a deep breath. "If you have a child by one of us, that baby will have a safe childhood filled with love and caring. When they come of age, only then, they will train with me until they are ready to take over leadership of the territory."

"What if they don't want to lead?"

I shrug. "Then I suppose they'll live a hopefully happy life until they die a peaceful death." Obviously that's not the preferred course of action, but forcing someone into a leadership position is a great way to ruin a territory. The best way to ensure we have a leader who wants the position is for Belladonna to bear several children while she's here, but I don't say as much now. She's already twisted up about the idea of a child. I told my court that we would be patient, and I mean to be exactly that.

Belladonna turns to look around the square, and I try to see things through her eyes. The buildings are all low and simple but expertly made. Once a week—and more often during the warmer months—we have a market where folks come in from the surrounding farmland and sell their excess produce and products, and there's a building designed for it, with stalls and the like, permanently set up opposite the manor. There is also a coffee and tea shop with small foodstuffs that people like to gather in, a clothing shop, a little health clinic, and a bakery. Farther out, there are lots of other shops and homes, but they can't be seen from here.

Belladonna finally turns to me, her brows drawn together in a frown. "Where is your church?"

I almost laugh; only the seriousness of her question stops me. "We don't worship any god you would recognize, darling—and when we *do* worship, it's doing what we do best."

She blinks slowly, as if debating asking the question I can see dancing on the tip of her tongue. Curiosity gets the best of her. "How do you worship?"

Even as I tell myself to keep my distance, the memory of her dream makes me reckless. I lean down until I can speak directly in her ear. "By fucking, love." Her surprise and curiosity and, yes, lust, have me elaborating. "The more pleasure given, the greater the worship. The more orgasms, the more satisfied our deity."

A little tremor works through her body, but she's stronger than she gives herself credit for. She doesn't crumple or flee. She just takes a careful inhale. "What deity wants worship like that?"

I force myself to ease back, to give her more breathing space. It won't do to rush this, to pressure her. I shrug. "They have no name, no form we can comprehend. Our god, if you want to call them that, is unknowable."

That cute little frown appears between her brows. "If they're unknowable, then how do you know that, uh, sex pleases them?"

I smile slowly, pleased at the way her pulse seems to increase in response. "Because, darling, it's what we were made for."

7

BELLADONNA

S ex as worship.

The very idea would have my mother reaching for her phone to call Pastor John, sure that demons had taken up residence inside me. Thinking about it should fill me with a shame that can only be combated with prayer and immediate repentance. And yet Rusalka says it as if it's fact. As if *of course* they worship their unknowable deity with sex, because that's what feels good and what they were made for. I'm not certain gods even exist, and now she's telling me that theirs wants them to have sex? It defies belief. "But do they know you're worshipping if they're unknowable? How do you know they're listening?"

"We don't. That's not what it's about."

I shake my head sharply. "That sounds like a cult."

She laughs, the sound deep and joyous. Everything about her seems deep and joyous. I don't understand it. Rusalka throws her arm around my shoulders as easily as if we've been friends for a lifetime. "Cults are a human creation, darling. All the people in my territory worship in the way they see fit, if they worship at all. It's hardly required, and each person can make their own decisions. Plenty of my people don't believe in deities at all. It's a varied experience. I'm not set up as their leader of their belief, only of their government."

The way she says it is so relaxed, as if it doesn't really matter if people believe in this deity or not. As if she truly doesn't care. It baffles me. "But what happens if they don't believe?"

"Nothing happens." Another shrug. She still has her arm around my shoulders, a warm and steady weight. She turns us back toward the manor, easily moving us away from the few people who still linger, watching me as if expecting me to save them. As if I've ever done anything but disappoint the people who expected things of me.

"But you just said . . ."

"I said they can choose. Just like *you* can choose. If you're not comfortable with the sex, then we won't expose you to it. I'll talk with my Insomnior Court and ensure they keep their activities behind closed doors."

My mind reels with all the information I've taken in, every bit of it conflicting with what has been drilled into me since childhood.

How many times have I harbored the thought that God, if He exists—They exist—must be larger than the hateful creature my parents' worship? Surely a god of that expansiveness doesn't care if I'm having premarital sex or masturbating. Surely if They paid that close of attention, all the atrocities in the world wouldn't happen. Surely my sister, a sweet and good person, shouldn't have gotten cancer.

I inhale Rusalka's spicy scent. Their warmth is a live thing against my side, flickering like a cozy fire through our clothes. It answers the question I'd barely allowed myself to think—their fire doesn't have to burn. There's a metaphor in that, but my mind is reeling too hard to divine it. "You need a baby."

"We'd like one eventually, yes." She urges me to start walking with the subtlest pressure. "But, as I've said before and will say again, it's not something you'll be forced or coerced into doing. We have time. There's no reason to rush things."

She's being too easy on me. I know what I signed up for. More than that, I'm starting to understand exactly what a child would mean to not only her, but every person who lives in this territory. "You said that either you or another would impregnate me. How does that work?" I wave at her hips and then realize I likely just overstepped dramatically. "That's too personal, isn't it? I'm sorry."

"There's nothing to be sorry for. As I said when we first met, my people tend to be fluid when it comes to gender. That doesn't simply mean how they identify. Most of us are shape-shifters on one level or another, which means we can generate the necessary appendage to get the job done."

" . . . Oh." I'm having a hard time wrapping my mind around that, so I set it aside for now. I think of the tears in the pregnant person's eyes, of the way their hope for the future practically shone from their face. I clear my throat. "How many succubi and incubi are there in your territory?"

"We don't keep a tight count, but somewhere north of three hundred thousand."

I stop short. *Three hundred thousand people.* "That's so many."

A shadow appears in her orange eyes. "There used to be many more, but each war has a cost, and my people are not fighters in the same way some of the others in this realm can be. We've suffered heavy losses over the generations."

I saw the dragon and the tentacled person and the

winged monster. All of them look stronger and more fear-some than Rusalka, at least physically. "And having a baby . . . a human leader . . . will benefit them all? That will protect them?"

"Yes. That will boost the naturally occurring magic in the territory. That helps crops grow, soothes the weather, makes it easier for our healers to do their jobs—all sorts of things." She speaks absently as she guides me up the manor steps and opens the door. "It's why my people elect the most powerful of us to be leader when the time comes. If the leader's magic starts to wane, then a new leader is chosen. We don't bother with bloodlines the way the other territo-ries do, and we've benefited as a result."

So many people. I could help *so many people*. Yes, the thought of having a child and leaving them behind hurts in a way I don't know how to conceptualize. But I've been dealing with hurt for my entire life. What's one more to add to the list, especially when the benefit is so expansive? "I'll do it."

Rusalka stops short. "Excuse me?"

"I'll have your baby—the baby. Whoever's baby. I consent."

She drops her arm and turns to study my face. I don't know what she sees there, but it doesn't seem to make her happy. Her gorgeous face is carefully blank, some of the fire in her deep-orange eyes banked. The banked fire feels like a loss, but I don't understand how I could lose something when I don't *have* anything.

Rusalka shakes her head. "That's not—"

Something snaps inside me. I'm so heartily tired of being told I don't know my own mind. "I would *very* much appreciate if you and Azazel and whoever else would stop telling me things I already know. I am aware I don't have to do anything I don't want to do. I *want* to help." All my life, I've never managed to measure up to anything, and now the only thing I have to do to help what I think is essentially a country full of people is the one thing I was taught was my purpose for existing.

Have a baby. And I don't even have to marry some man who's supposed to lead the relationship and shove me into a box that seems designed to suffocate me.

Rusalka tenses like she's going to keep arguing, but she finally nods slowly. I can't help sweeping my gaze over her. We've only been around each other for a day, and I'm already getting used to how perfectly the nonhuman parts of her meld with the rest of her. None of the demons I've seen depicted in church were feminine—none of the angels, either, now that I think of it—but if ever there was a person created to tempt me . . .

But I don't really believe that, do I? Rusalka may be a literal succubus, but even with her powers of seduction, she's shown me more care than most people I've known my entire life. More care than Ruth, even, because the only thing Rusalka questions is my decision to have a baby, not every element of my very existence.

She takes a deep breath. "If that's still your choice at the end of the week, then I'll honor it." She holds up one black claw before I can protest. "We have seven years, Belladonna. One week is a small enough ask to make."

"But—"

"I would like you to join me tonight for some entertainment." They don't give me a chance to respond. It feels like one moment I'm trying to find the words to tell them that I don't need a week to make my decision, and the next Rusalka is stopping in front of my room and laying their hands on my shoulders. They peer down at me, as if searching for the answer to a question I don't understand.

Rusalka presses a light kiss to my forehead. It's a touch that should feel innocent—it's certainly far from any known pleasure zones—but it goes through me like a tornado of fire. I shiver and stare up at them. "What are you doing to me?"

"Nothing." She smiles slowly. "Yet."

8

RUSALKA

The moment I open the door to my bedroom, I register that I'm not alone. In the beat it takes to draw my powers around me, encircle my body in flames, a figure steps out of my closet, one of my favorite dresses draped over their arm. I recognize them immediately—Ramanu, one of Azazel's pet bargainer demons, high enough up the chain of command that they wouldn't dare trespass without explicit permission.

They smile and turn unerringly to face me despite the horns that curl from where eye sockets would be if they had eyes. It doesn't seem to matter that they can't see in the traditional sense. They make a good production of it. "Put away the fireworks, Rusalka."

I dampen the heat but don't withdraw it completely. "What are you doing here?"

"Checking up on Azazel's contracted human, of course." Their grin turns sharp and cutting. "It was in the fine print."

"I read the contract." I finish stepping into the room and close the door. "But you won't find Belladonna in my bedroom, and you certainly won't find her wearing *that* dress." It's a filmy thing, meant to seduce, falling in sensual lines from the neck to the floor—and completely transparent.

If I wear that dress, it might give Belladonna a stroke from fighting her desire for me. No doubt there would be some nonsense about leading the others around her into sin. I'm still not sure if I want to alchemize that shame into something hot and fiery or if I want to dig it out with my claws. I can count the time I've spent with her in mere hours, and yet it bothers me down to my core how much she hurts for the sake of others.

Her lived experience is so different from mine. I grew up wanting for nothing—certainly not love—and willingly stepped into this leadership position. I was a full adult, more than able to assess the cost, and I judged the sacrifices I would be called to make as worthy, benefiting the lives of many. We are not the same . . .

There's still something about her that makes it feel like she's staring at me, holding up a warped mirror.

"Pity. It would look as stunning on her as it no doubt does on you." Ramanu tosses the dress carelessly onto my bed. "Interesting that you're already so protective of her."

"Of course I am," I snap. They're trying to get under my skin. I know better than to engage, but Belladonna has me too on edge to play word games. "She's fine. Ready to martyr herself to serve a territory of people she doesn't know."

"Hmmm." Ramanu gives a show of examining their claws, so similar to mine. They are supposedly the product of a bargainer demon and a gargoyle, but I suspect there's a stray succubi or incubi in their family history as well.

I shake my head, already tired of this. "Spit it out, Ramanu. You're no fool. If you wanted to talk to Belladonna, it's easy enough to seek her out. You're in *my* bedroom for a reason."

"Maybe I'm here to seduce you."

I burst out laughing. It feels good, a release of the pressure that's been building since I brought a fatalistic human into my territory. "Darling, we've traveled those roads before, and while you were a thoroughly enjoyable partner, I think it's safe to say that neither of us is interested in retreading that territory." I suspect they have someone they're interested in for more than mere sex, and that's not something I could give them, even if they wanted it. Which they didn't We work better as friends. The last thing I need is Azazel thinking he has some hold over me because I'm sleeping with one of his demons.

They give a chuckle of their own. "True enough."

"Glad we got that out of the way." I cross my arms over my chest and let my flames fade away. "I'm listening."

"You're not normally so abrupt." They perch on the edge of my bed.

"And somehow, you're always this coy."

They sigh. "Azazel is worried about the girl."

"I'm aware. We spoke before the choosing." It irks me that he's sent his babysitter so quickly, but it's not unexpected. Belladonna is everything Azazel feared and more. I still can't quite believe she made the impulsive decision to bear a child for my territory. I should be elated. That theoretical child represents a safety and prosperity unlike any we've seen in my lifetime.

Bu it doesn't feel right.

A week still isn't long enough to make it feel right, but I suspect it's as much time as I can get away with before she balks at the delay.

"So much conflict." Ramanu waves their hand through

the air as if testing currents. Due to their gargoyle parent, they can read auras, similar to how I can read desires and emotions. I was taught to shield, just like all children, but there's no point in trying to with Ramanu. They're here for an accurate report, after all. I have nothing to hide. "So much need."

"*Ramanu.*"

"The contract states no harm may come to the human. Azazel is concerned that it won't recognize harm in the traditional manner, because of her . . . history."

"He's right to be concerned." I should watch my words, should keep my conflict to the Insomnior Court, where I know it won't go beyond those walls. "She agreed to have a child."

Ramanu's perfect coy persona flickers, true shock showing. "So quickly."

"Yes."

"And yet you're not exuberant."

I can't hold still any longer. I pace from one side of the room to the other, my long legs eating up the distance before the motion can satisfy the tumult inside me. "It's wrong. It would be taking advantage."

"It would help your territory. Isn't that your end all, be all?"

I snap a look at them. "Don't act the part of a hurt lover now, Ramanu. You were no more invested in our fling than I was."

"It's true." They shrug. "But so is the fact that you have gone to extreme and occasionally harmful lengths to be a good leader to your people. Far beyond what other leaders do."

"That just makes them poor leaders," I snap.

"I see." They nod slowly and rise to their feet. "What will you do?"

"Scare the shit out of her." I hold up a hand when they tense. "Not like that. Give me some credit. She's so twisted up, she doesn't know what she's feeling at any given time. She *wants*, Ram—it fills up a room—but the shame she feels chokes it near to death."

They lean forward, interest lighting up their pretty features and warming their crimson skin. "You're going to seduce her."

"Not yet." I want her. Gods, I want her. More than I could have anticipated, even after that delicious dream. Me, who can find something worth desiring in any partner. Belladonna *aches*, and I ache in time with her. "I'm going to bring her to a play party with a handful of trusted friends. Observing only."

This time their chuckle is full-bodied and fills up the room. "That's going to blow her mind."

"Likely." I'll have to pay close attention in order to ensure it doesn't push her over the edge. I'm well aware that the price for harming Belladonna is my territory, but that's not my sole motivation for being careful.

A good leader is ruthless, yes, and cunning, but they don't trample on people more fragile than they are. Doing so damages a community—do it enough and there's no community left to speak of, nothing to protect. If more leaders took that truth to heart, there would be less sorrow in the dreams of humans I visit.

Ramanu sighs, some of their amusement filtering away. "Seems like you have things well in hand."

"Don't sound so disappointed that there's no drama to stir up." Their propensity to wreak havoc is part of what first drew me to them. Life is rarely boring when Ramanu is making an appearance. I motion to the door. "She's in her room if you want to check in on her."

"And traumatize the poor thing further? Between the horns and my humor, she's unlikely to recover in her current state." They laugh. "I think not. Let her settle in a bit more. I'll return at a later date." They pause. "But, truly, congratulations, Rusalka. I know what this will mean for you."

I shake my head. "Don't congratulate me yet."

Ramanu grins. "That right there is why I am. You'll do right by her. I have no doubt about that."

I don't ask about the other territory leaders, though curiosity threatens to sink its teeth into me. I may not know them on a personal level, but I know how they operate. Some of them will fare better with their humans than others. Still, Ramanu's confidence in me smoothes something jagged in my chest. "Thank you."

"Wear that dress for your party." Their smile goes mischievous. "If she doesn't have a heart attack from shock, she won't be able to keep her hands off you." There's a slight pop as the air pressure changes, and then Ramanu is gone.

I glare at the space they just occupied, but the expression is half-hearted. "Dramatic to the bitter end." I move to my bed and pick up the dress they tossed there, then run my claws carefully over the slick fabric. They're right, of course. This dress is meant to seduce and may even be enough for Belladonna to forget her shame and see what it could be like on the other side . . .

It's perfect.

9

BELLADONNA

I keep expecting Rusalka to return, but they don't. Not through the long afternoon hours where the sun creates lazy beams through the window that I can hear people moving about the square through. Not as the sky deepens to a dusky blue color and stars begin to appear. Not when dinner is brought to my door by a cranky, short woman named Jitka who demands I eat the whole plate before leaving and slamming the door behind her.

That makes me wonder if I've upset Rusalka.

No, that's not the truth.

I *know* I've upset them.

I want to pretend I don't know why, to cling to some indignation at the fact that I'm giving her what she wants and now she doesn't want it. That would be false indignation.

Rusalka is a good person. Maybe I haven't known her long enough to make that claim unilaterally, but it's hard to argue otherwise. In the same situation, my parents and Pastor John wouldn't have hesitated to accept my sacrifice as their due. Even Ruth wouldn't question the necessity of it, though it might bring her more sorrow than she'd show to anyone but me. Of course one person sacrificing to benefit the whole is the way to go. Of course we don't need to worry about that single person. They're doing the right thing.

I'm so distracted, I can't even enjoy the rainbow of clothes that showed up in my wardrobe while I was out this morning. I'm nearly certain they're the same as those options from Azazel's castle, which raises questions I'm not sure I'm brave enough to ask.

I manage to pull on a pretty deep-red dress with an overlay that floats around me as if by magic and a fitted, shorter sheath bottom layer. Even as I pull my hair up into some semblance of order, I pretend I didn't pick the dress because it's red and made me think of Rusalka. I tell myself I don't care what they think of it.

In short, I lie.

A knock on my door has my heart leaping into my throat. I rush over and throw it open, but my smile fades as I don't find the person I'm most looking forward to seeing.

Instead, there. are two strangers. One is a few inches taller than me and has dark-brown skin, an athletic body, and flames flickering around their form. Succubus, then. They wear loose black pants that taper to their hooves and an equally loose gray shirt with a daring deep V that leaves most of their chest exposed.

The other is nearly as tall as Rusalka, with a mass of dark curls that seems to move in a wind I don't feel and skin that's a patterned combination of medium brown and a color pale enough to be termed literally white. I know what this is called. It takes a moment for the term to come to me —vitiligo. No flames to be seen. Is this an incubus? They have on a flowing set of robes in a deep orange that simultaneously shows off and hides a curvy body depending on how they move.

I realize I'm staring and clear my throat. "Hello."

"You *are* a pretty little thing, aren't you?" The curly-haired one takes a step toward me, but the succubus pulls them back. They give the succubus a pouting look. "I was just being friendly."

"Save it for the party." The dark-haired one turns to me and offers their arm. "I'm Danik. This is Zhenya."

Zhenya jerks a thumb at Danik. "He/him." They point to themselves. "Ze/zir. Rusalka said you would ask."

To my shame, I'm already so overwhelmed, I don't know if I would have *remembered* to ask.

They're both beautiful in a way I don't know how to define. It's not necessarily the kind of beauty I grew up feeling shame from wanting to strive for—too sharp, too off-kilter—but it draws me all the same. "I'm Belladonna," I finally manage.

"We know." Zhenya doesn't say it unkindly. Ze smiles. "Come play with us, pretty human."

I set my hand on Danik's arm in a daze. "It's nice to meet you."

"So polite." Danik's smile is a little too wicked to be comforting. It makes my whole body go tight. I try to fight the feeling; it feels like a betrayal to Rusalka. From the way his smile widens, he senses my desire the same way Rusalka always seems to.

I'm too overwhelmed to come up with a response as they escort me down the hall to the stairs. This house is larger than any I've been in to date, Azazel's castle excepted. It looks like something out of a movie, all luxurious carpet and deep greens on the walls and brown of the trim. The stairs are wide and curving and take us down to the foyer. There, we turn inward again, and go through yet more halls to a wide set of double doors.

Inside, the air smells of cloves and cinnamon, and it's several degrees warmer than the rest of the house. There are strangely shaped couches and chairs arranged around the area, and a large chest is tucked in the corner near a wardrobe that's easily twice the size of the one in my room.

"This will be fun, Belladonna. Don't worry." Zhenya drops onto one of the wavy couches, exposing one smooth thigh that morphs into hooves the same deep black that both succubi and incubi seem to have. Ze turns on zir side and props zir head on one hand. "Sit down. Danik will get you a drink."

"I don't really drink," I say faintly. It's one of those holdovers from the church, even though my reasoning for it now is less sin-related and more because I don't like feeling out of control.

Zhenya waves that away. "No mind-altering substances for our darling human, don't worry. Rusalka wants you in your right mind—at least initially."

I don't know what to say to that, because Danik is here, pressing a flute of some bubbly liquid into my hand. I take a cautious sip. "Oh wow." It's as spicy as the air smells— almost painful on my tongue, but in a good way. It confuses me, so I take another drink. "What is this?"

"It has a lot of names, but it's essentially faerie wine," Danik says.

"Without all the fun side effects," Zhenya cuts in, still sounding on the verge of laughter. "We *do* have the more interesting version, but it's for special occasions."

"That's . . . nice." I'm saved from saying something else by the doors opening again and another person coming through. This one is as short as me, with pale skin and deep-crimson hair and eyes. They smile sweetly at me, but my attention is caught by the person closing the door softly behind them.

Rusalka.

They look mouthwatering in a black dress as sheer as the overlay I'm wearing and in a similar style. The only difference between how we're dressed is that there's nothing underneath it.

Even as I tell myself to look away, I can't help tracing the long lines of her body—so strong and beautiful—from the curve of her waist to the fullness of her breasts. I can see her *nipples*.

She crosses to me in a few smooth steps and takes my hands. "You look amazing, darling."

I part my lips, but I can't seem to speak.

Rusalka smiles. "Now that you've met Danik and Zhenya, let me introduce you to Inna. They're the final member of my Insomnior Court, and I trust them all with my life—and yours. If you ever need something and I'm not available, don't hesitate to reach out to one of them."

I know I should be processing their words, but I'm so enamored with Rusalka's beauty that I'm having a hard time following. "Oh."

She squeezes my hands. "Come sit. Let us welcome you to the territory properly." There's a thread in their tone, something sensual and inviting, but I don't know how to divine exactly what it means.

She leads me to a wide chair and, to my surprise and delight, sinks down next to me and drapes one long arm over the back of the chair. We end up pressed together from knee to shoulder, her warmth making me shiver. I glance up at her, but her attention is on the other three, her smile now soft and amused. "Shall we begin?"

"Don't rush me." Zhenya has a bit of a pout in zir voice, but ze rises and, with one practiced motion, drops zir robe. I can't help my gasp as I stare at zir beauty. Gentle curves, stretch marks, dimpled skin, and a radiance that makes me dizzy. When I finally drag my gaze back to zir face, ze is grinning. "Oh, I *like* her."

"Focus," Rusalka says mildly.

Zhenya ignores her and strolls over to stand before me. Even this close, I can't tell if ze smells different than the room or if zir proximity is increasing the clove scent hanging heavy in the air. Ze props zir hands on zir hips. "We're going to have such fun together, Belladonna. Just wait."

I don't know if I'm supposed to notice zir genitals. I can't help it. They're directly even with my face, the apex of their thighs an invitation that the ugly little voices in the back of my mind are screaming at me to ignore. I clear my voice. "What . . . What should I . . . ?"

"Rusalka, she's so polite." Zhenya laughs, but it's not like ze is laughing at me, more like ze is inviting me to be included in the joke. "May I?"

"Don't ask me." There's a new edge to Rusalka's voice. "Belladonna is our guest, and you are obviously intent on trampling on my plans for the night." She waves a graceful hand, giving permission.

Zhenya leans down while gripping the back of the chair with one hand, bracketing me into my seat. "May I, Belladonna?" The playfulness hasn't disappeared from zir voice, but there's so much more there.

I don't know what ze is asking me, but I suddenly want it desperately. "Yes."

"Good girl," ze purrs. Ze takes my hand and presses it to zir full chest. "Chest." Ze pauses, as if waiting for me to pull away, but I'm mesmerized by zir softness. Ze slowly traces my hand down zir round stomach and stops just south of zir belly button. "Sex."

"Oh." I swallow past my suddenly dry throat. "Um, thank you." Rusalka is *right there*, and I'm touching another person in a way that can't be defined as anything other than sexual. I dart a look at her, but instead of looking jealous or angry, she seems . . . intrigued.

"Thank *you*, sweet girl." Zhenya rises, causing my fingertips to brush over zir sex, then releases me. "Inna prefers the terms 'chest' and 'cock' for their body. Danik as well." Ze turns and walks back to the couch, a swivel in zir step that makes me squirm in my seat.

I want Rusalka. I'm not supposed to desire more people. Wanting *her* is complicated enough. Apparently I am just as bad as my parents always said, just as eager to fall into sin. No, damn it, *no*. I don't believe what they believe, and I refuse to let their hate ruin the party Rusalka set up for me. Even so, I can't help looking at her. "I'm sorry," I whisper.

"Lust is natural, darling." Rusalka twines a strand of my hair around their claw. "Acting on it is pure and good as long as it's consensual. Zhenya loves to show off, and everyone in my court shares one another's bed from time to time, as well as has sex with others. As long as everyone is in agreement about expectations, then no harm done." She tugs a little, just hard enough to make a dull ache rise in my scalp. "But I'll be put out if you fall face-first into someone else's sex before I get a taste of yours."

My skin heats and then heats more, until I feel like an

inferno just below the surface. Out of the corner of my eye, I see Zhenya giggle and Danik say something, but I can't tear my gaze from Rusalka. "You want me?"

She gives an exasperated sigh. "*Yes*, Belladonna. And not simply for what you can give me—but for what *I* can give *you*. Now, settle in and enjoy the show."

10

RUSALKA

When I agreed to this deal with Azazel, I didn't expect to feel so conflicted. I figured it would be an easy thing to manage this strange human's tendency to commit to actions that would harm her. Simple. Then I met Belladonna and realized the strength of the metaphorical demons riding her no matter how hard she tries to escape them.

My girl doesn't exactly want to be a martyr, but she seems to feel she doesn't have any other choice.

Now she sits next to me, shivering in some combination of trepidation and want, as Zhenya straddles Danik and leans over to kiss Inna. Incubi and succubi can't feed from one another the way we can feed from human dreams, but we're all hedonists at heart. We love pleasure for pleasure's sake, and no one gives pleasure like my Insomnior Court.

It's impossible to relax with Belladonna's conflicting desires practically screaming in my ear. I finally twist to face her. "There's no shame in this." I try to say this gently but can't help the sharpness in my words.

"Are they . . ." She swallows visibly. "Are they polyamorous? That's what it's called, right?"

"Danik is mated to a fellow succubus, and he isn't romantically involved with either Zhenya or Inna."

Belladonna turns those bright eyes my way. "He looks involved right now."

"Pleasure isn't taboo. There are those among my people who prefer to be monogamous, but many of the mated pairs choose not to be. His mate, Feofan, openly encourages him to find his pleasure where he may, and he does the same." I tamp down on the tiny sliver of impatience I feel at explaining something as common as gravity. It's not Belladonna's fault that the other territories look down on us for this practice or that they reduce it to something of a joke. That's not why she's asking the question. She doesn't understand. I can't expect her to.

"But . . ." She presses her lips together.

"Ask."

"But what about children? What if someone gets pregnant or gets someone pregnant that isn't their mate?"

Again, I swallow past my instinctive snapping response. There's no cut in her question, just genuine confusion and curiosity. I take a slow breath. "Children are sacred, Belladonna. We don't have them as often as our ancestors did."

"Why not?"

"There are a number of theories, but the most prominent among them is that with each generation, the human elements in our bloodlines grow thinner, and our propensity for plentiful procreation decreases in relation." I rush on before she can offer to have a child again to fix that. "However a child comes about—and it's always a choice, not a requirement—they're a blessing. They are welcomed with open arms. Not only the biological parents are parents to them. We all are."

"I don't understand." Her gaze tracks to where Inna has pulled off Danik's pants and is sucking his cock deep into their throat. "I don't understand any of this."

She may not understand it, but she isn't trying to fight the spell of desire being cast in the room. She almost melts into my side. I study her profile. "Do you have to understand in order to accept?"

"I don't know." She sighs and rests her head on my shoulder, the move so trusting that my stomach lodges in my throat. "I want this, Rusalka. I want this freedom, this . . . *joy*. I just don't know how to take it. Every time I even think of trying, I have a chorus of voices in my head yelling at me that I'm going to burn in hell. I'm not even sure I believe in hell, and yet I can't shake the fear."

I tell myself to be patient, to wait, to coax her out of her shell of shame in a way only time can manage, but I can't help responding to the desperation in her tone. "I can make them go quiet."

"I want that."

Across the room, Zhenya moans as Inna pushes two fingers into zir while they keep sucking Danik's cock. The sound curls through me, an invitation and more. Normally, I would be in the midst of them already, stroking and touching and riling the entire group to new heights.

Instead, I'm sitting next to a quivering human who doesn't know how to take what she wants and offering something I have no business offering. "It's similar to what I did in your dream. I can magically . . . smooth things over . . . if you want me to. It will be a bit like being drunk or high. Everything will feel good, and you won't want it to stop."

The moment Belladonna draws in a sharp breath, I know what her answer will be. "Do it."

"Belladonna . . ." I sigh. It's my fault for even bringing it up. "Are you sure that's what you want?"

"Yes." She grabs my arm, her hand shaking. "Yes, please. It's what I *need*."

"First, ground rules." I cup her cheek when she tries to turn away. "I understand the way shame feels like it's holding you down, holding you back. But consent is nonnegotiable, little one. You won't want to stop once I release your inhibitions, so we need to know where we have to stop for you."

She blinks those big dark eyes at me and turns to where my friends and lovers are now fully naked and alternating between moans and giggles, the latter sound being Inna's— they always giggle when they come. I allow the turn, allow her to see them in their glory.

Belladonna focuses back on me. "I want everything."

"Easy to say, harder to understand." I stroke my thumb over her cheekbone. "Tonight we'll keep things simple enough. Penetrative sex?"

Her eyes get bigger. "Yes," she whispers.

"Mmm." I drag my fingertips along her jaw. I should stop for this conversation, shouldn't be touching her at all, but I can't seem to help myself when she leans so sweetly against my touch. "Oral sex?"

"Yes." Belladonna quivers. "Please."

"Kissing?"

"Yes."

"Penetration of your mouth, your pussy, your pretty little ass?"

Her quivering becomes shaking, but she nods sharply. "All of it. *Everything*, Rusalka. I want everything."

"That will cover tonight's activities." Even with verbal consent, I shouldn't do this. Fool that I am, I can't deny her. I lean in and press a soft kiss to her full lips. It's a relatively chaste touch, one completely devoid of tongue, but I use the contact to press my power into her. It bumps up against her shame and then slides beneath and flowers inside her.

The tension bleeds out of her body instantly. She tangles her fingers in my hair and presses harder against me. *"Oh."* Belladonna laughs, the sound free and light and stabbing me directly in the chest. She tilts back just enough to press her fingers to her lips. "I didn't know it could be like that."

I'm not a particularly violent person—there are a thousand better ways to get what you want—but seeing the wonder bloom on her face makes me want to hunt down everyone who warped her concept of pleasure and love to remove them from existence. Shame kills as certainly as a knife. It's harder to identify—a person can keep walking around while they're dead inside—but no less real.

She leans forward to kiss me again, but I urge her to stand. "Go play, little one. Enjoy yourself."

She pouts, all playful disappointment. "But I want to play with *you*."

Fire sprouts around me, an external response to my need to give her exactly that. I want her. Desperately. She's beautiful and kind and far too selfless. I could teach my sweet little human to be selfish, just a little, just enough to take care of herself. To *demand* the pleasure she's due.

I simply . . . don't want it like this.

My fire flickers in her dark-brown eyes and is evident in the way she presses her thighs together, in how she licks her lips. My magic can't create desire where there is none—my girl wants me—but, though I don't fault her this, I don't want her when she has to be blitzed to act on wanting me back.

Romantic fool.

I ignore my own self-condemnation and turn Belladonna around to face my Insomnior Court. "Go, little one."

She flounces. It's the cutest thing I've ever seen, and each bouncing step makes her ass jiggle. My mouth waters. I want to explore every inch of her with my tongue. I want to banish my court from the room and keep her all to myself. I want to turn her loose at one of the large parties just to see what mischief she would get up to. I *want*.

But I don't do any of that.

Instead of going to the couch with the others to sink into them, I cross one leg over the other and lean back. I'm used to wanting. It makes desire sweeter to be denied.

11

BELLADONNA

E very single time I've even *thought* about sex has come with a lash of knowing I shouldn't. Shouldn't lust, shouldn't fantasize, certainly shouldn't touch myself. Even when I push back and try to fight it, that feeling of *shouldn't* is still there, whispering in the back of my mind. Right now, it's completely drowned out by the liquid heat in my body.

The *need*.

"Come here, pretty human." Zhenya is breathless, probably because ze is on Danik's cock, rocking in a way that makes my thighs shake.

I cast a glance over my shoulder at Rusalka, but they haven't moved from their spot on the wide couch. They lounge like I imagine a monarch would, one long leg draped over the arm of the chair, their chin in their hand, amusement and interest in every line of their perfect body.

Is there a word stronger than "need"? There must be, to encapsulate the overwhelming urge I have to turn fully back to them, to kneel before them, to beg them to touch me, fuck me, go down the same list they used earlier, checking off boxes along the way.

But Rusalka waves those long black-tipped fingers at the trio behind me. A clear order. An order that makes my stomach hot and squirmy.

I turn and accept Inna's waiting hand, allowing them to pull me into Zhenya's arms. It's sensory overload. All three of them are so beautiful, so soft, smell so good, it threatens to overwhelm me, even with Rusalka's magic propelling me.

"Go slow with our precious Belladonna," Zhenya says, a playful flirtation in zir voice. Ze cups my face, still rocking on Danik's cock, and pulls me down for a light kiss. It's nearly the same move Rusalka made, but it feels drastically different. Good, but . . . different.

That doesn't stop heat from blooming inside me as if ze fanned flames I can't see. The sensation only gets stronger when Inna presses against my back and draws my hair to the side, baring my neck. They lean in and inhale deeply. "You smell decadent."

Each touch, each brush of their lips against my exposed skin, further quiets the voices in my head that I never wanted to claim as my own. I feel light and free for the first time in my life. Is this what being drunk is like? Maybe I should have tried it a long time ago.

I lean back against Inna, a giggle slipping from my lips. "This is wild."

"Darling, you have no idea." Rusalka's voice wraps around me as if she's reached across the distance and stroked her claws down my sternum. It makes me shiver harder. I like what the others are doing to me. I like it a *lot*, but I want her.

Inna keeps kissing my neck, their fangs pricking my skin even as their tongue soothes the tiny pain. It makes me jump and jolt and shake as if I'm no longer in control of my body. I'm not certain I am.

"May I?" This from Danik, whose hand is snaking around Zhenya's waist toward me.

"Yes." The word is out almost before he has a chance to finish speaking.

He brushes his knuckles over my stomach in a downward motion.

Zhenya's hands join his, and they pull at the fabric of my dress. At least until a soft sound from Rusalka makes both of them pause. I can't see her from my current position. That feels wrong, somehow. Unacceptable. "I want to see," I murmur.

Zhenya laughs. "Of course you do."

Inna tugs me out of Zhenya's grasp and guides me to a spot on the couch next to Danik. He catches my hand, raises it to his lips, and brushes a kiss against my knuckles. My gaze follows the movement, then continues to where his eyes glow a deep orange. That should scare me, maybe. But how can I be scared when the heat there is all lust and no threat?

Danik nods to Rusalka. Her eyes glow, perfect twins to his, but despite the beautiful people arranged around me, all mostly naked, her attention seems to be on *me*. Flames flicker around her, twining with her pale hair and licking across her exposed shoulders. I was too nervous before to fully comprehend the masterpiece that is her dress. I can *see* her.

Inna kneels in front of me, a distraction I don't know if I'm grateful or resentful for. They don't give me a chance to decide. They shift forward, pressing my legs wide, and run their hands up my outer thighs. My dress is long enough that they're not touching bare skin, but this is closer than

I've been to anyone other than . . . Well, the less said about my sole sexual experience, the better.

Shadows flicker over their pale skin and meld together over their hands. Their eyes lean closer to red than orange, but the same desire that's in Danik's gaze, in Zhenya's, is here with Inna. Their hands stop at the tops of my thighs, the slight pressure of their claws through my dress a promise of more to come. "May I?"

There's only one answer. There's only ever been one answer. This feels good. We've barely done anything, but this still feels *so good*. There's no talk of *we shouldn't* or *what will people think?* or any kind of judgment about the destination we're clearly headed to. It's free in a way I still can't fully comprehend.

But as I answer, it's Rusalka's gaze I meet. "Yes."

Her lips curve, whether in approval or amusement, I can't begin to say. I don't get a chance to find out, not when Inna dips forward and presses their mouth to my center. The slick silk between their tongue and my heated flesh is barely any barrier at all.

The touch jolts me out of my pleasant inebriation— barely. It lingers at the edges, soothing me into lust-filled relaxation, but the question demands an answer. I stare down at them, my mouth hanging open, my eyes far too wide. "Wh-what?"

They stop instantly and lift their head to look at me. "I'm sorry. You said yes, so I thought . . ." They shake their head. "I'll stop."

"No!" I make an effort to compose myself, but how am I supposed to be composed when I know *that* is an option? Of course I've read about oral sex, of course I agreed to it when Rusalka went down her list, but somehow in all the fantasizing, I never realized it would be like this. "Please don't stop."

With my consent, the sensation of magic settles back over me once more.

"If you're—"

"She was clear, Inna." Rusalka examines her claws.

There's a new tension in her body now. Is she angry? Did I do something wrong? I must have. She arranged this lovely experience for me, and I'm ruining it.

Before I can figure out what I'm supposed to say, Inna dips back down and covers me with their mouth. This time, there's no hesitation, no doubt. They lick me through the fabric as it becomes wet with my need. Slick. Slippery.

"Relax, sweet girl." Zhenya moved while I was distracted, shifted to face Danik as ze rocked on his cock. Ze leans toward me and smooths my hair away from my face. It's a downright sweet gesture, somehow not remotely at odds with the way Inna has parted my folds and is gently rolling their tongue against my clitoris. "Let Inna take care of you."

How can sex be *care*?

I can't find the breath to ask the question. Not with Zhenya's claws stroking over me. Not with Danik draping one long arm over my shoulders, tucking me against his body even as tension weaves through me, tighter and tighter. He's . . . anchoring me. Keeping me steady even as I unravel.

Inna urges one of my legs up and over their shoulder, spreading me wider. My dress is a laughable barrier between us, but they make no move to remove it. Instead, they seem to savor this act of giving just as much as I'm savoring the act of receiving.

In the midst of this, my gaze finds Rusalka again.

She doesn't appear to have moved an inch, but there's something tense about her, as if she's about to spring into motion. As if she's holding herself back.

That won't do. "I need . . ." I lift my hand to reach for her, to beg her to join, but then Inna's fangs prick my skin through the fabric on either side of my clit and pleasure *explodes* inside me.

My back bows, and my head slams back into Danik's arm. Zhenya catches my arms and murmurs soothing words. She presses kisses along my jaw, and Inna just keeps working me with their tongue even as their teeth seem to sprout delicious flames inside my skin.

It's too much. I can't—I don't—

I think I scream. Maybe I cry out Rusalka's name. It's all a blur until blessed darkness takes me.

12

RUSALKA

The moment Belladonna orgasms, I wonder if this is a mistake. Because it should be *my* mouth urging her to new heights, *my* claws scraping gently over her skin, *my* arm holding her steady as she comes apart.

And yet, it can't be me.

Because even now, I'm fighting the urge to tell my court to keep going, to see if we can draw another of those sweet cries from her lips, to see if she really did scream *my* name as she orgasmed. To urge her to do it again and again.

At the same time, I want to rip into them. To tear them away from her for daring to coax unrestrained pleasure from her when that's all I want. I can't decide if this is because I haven't tasted and touched Belladonna properly yet, or because I've suddenly started to see the advantage to monogamy. Either way, it would be the wrong call.

She just had a life-altering experience, and pushing her too far, too fast will harm her. Allowing my jealousy to slip its leash is dangerous, too; she's likely to misread it and think I'm judging her for the pleasure she just embraced.

It's right and good that Inna is slowly easing their ministrations and stroking her thighs soothingly. That Zhenya is pressing a tender kiss to her lips before ze resumes the rhythm that will send zir over the edge as well. That Danik squeezes Belladonna's shoulder comfortingly, continuing to offer his steady support, even as he grips Zhenya's hip and urges zir faster.

Belladonna is limp, but her energy is good, smooth and relaxed. The orgasm will dispel the magic, and I want her to come down softly before that damned shame rears its ugly head.

I could leave her here to my court's tender care. I trust them implicitly, even in this, even with her, but the strange jealousy is threatening to take root in the base of my spine, is spiraling upward and threatening to take over my mouth. It doesn't make sense. Jealousy can be a delightful edge to introduce into sex games, but it has no purpose beyond that. I have shared every partner I've ever had, happy that there were others who could meet their physical and emotional needs because my main priority has always been being a good leader. Doing so means being a shitty partner, but with good communication, most of my past lovers have been understanding of my emotional limits. Belladonna isn't even truly my partner to feel possessive over. It's disconcerting in the extreme.

That doesn't stop me from rising and crossing to sink down on her other side.

Inna moves back, shifting over to Danik and Zhenya, then Inna grins at me, their eyes too knowing. "We'll be going for a while yet, and I took the liberty of inviting more to join us once you've tucked our delightful Belladonna into bed." Their smile goes tender. "You were right to pick her."

"I know." I scoop Belladonna's limp body into my arms

just as she begins to stir. She's too fucking cute, nuzzling against my throat. It makes me tighten my grip on her. It makes me want . . . A lot of things.

Instead I summon a wicked smile for my Insomnior Court. "Have fun, my darlings." Then I stride out of the room without looking back. Voices whisper from downstairs, the invited guests. I pick up the tones of Feofan, two incubi who have been courting Zhenya—and each other—and several others I can't immediately place. It will be a party, indeed.

Any other night, I would be eager to rejoin them and immerse myself in the varied pleasures offered. I would be *impatient* to return to the room and the temporary escape it offered, at least for a few hours, before I needed to get back to work. Instead, I slow my steps, taking my time as I make my way to Belladonna's room. Prolonging the comfort of holding her in my arms.

Even with the leisurely pace, I still reach her room far too soon. "You can open your eyes, little one. I know you're back with me."

She obeys, just like she always seems to. I expect her to drop her eyes, to hide from me, but when I look down, she's studying my face as if attempting to memorize every line and curve. She wets her lips. "You gave me a long list, I said yes to all of it, and they didn't even take my clothes off."

"Yes." I shift my grip on her so I can open the door.

"But . . . why?"

As if on cue, her shame arises in a wave meant to kill the unwary, unseeable as it is. I press my lips to her temple but don't set her down. "What part of what happened is causing you to feel this way?"

She parts her lips like she might lie but finally shifts

uncomfortably in my arms and says, "I liked that you watched. I liked imagining it was *your* mouth on me."

My knees go a little weak, but I'm not leader of this territory through sheer charisma alone. A leader must learn when to dissemble and when to be explicitly honest. Showing Belladonna my shock would only reinforce her shame. So I merely smile. "I want that, too."

"Then why—" She cuts herself off, shakes her head sharply, then seems to force herself to continue. "Why not do it?"

There's no good reason to keep holding her, so I set her on her feet, even though I can't quite manage to release her. I skate my hands over her hips and then cup her elbows. She smells of sex, a growing need, and something floral that I can't quite place.

In that moment, when I finally meet her gaze, I don't see unrestricted desire there. If I had, I don't know that I would've remembered myself enough to avoid kissing her. But that's not what I see. There's desire, yes, and need so strong that I can't help leaning toward her.

And, underneath it all, a shame so thick that I want to spit and clear its taste from my mouth.

"Because." It takes conscious effort to release her, to step back, to allow the air to rush into the new space between us. "I want you, Belladonna. Desperately, in fact. You're beautiful and you're kind and you're strong. Not to mention your desire is strong enough to drown cities."

Her cheeks deepen into a crimson color against her tan skin. "Then why not take me?"

Gods, if she understood the effect her words have on me.

I clear my throat. It does nothing to negate the knot forming there because the knot isn't real. It's all emotion, messy and illogical. "Because, little one." My voice is raspy, but I can't help it. "Because, when I take you, I want you fully in possession of your faculties—not lust drunk on my power. I want your need for me to overpower the shame your people have cursed you with."

"Cursed." She frowns. "It does feel like a curse, doesn't it?"

"You would know better than I." For all my experience with humans' dreaming selves, I'm still an observer. I can see the desires, see the things blocking those desires, but I'm not the one experiencing them. I'm not a mind reader. I can't reach into Belladonna's soul and pull her shame out at its poisonous root.

She rubs her chest as if she can feel my violent desire. "It was so *easy* in there. I knew what I wanted, and I went for it. I didn't doubt."

"I know."

She ducks her head, letting her hair fall forward and hiding her expression from me. "I want you, Rusalka. I want you so desperately, it feels like a spell, even though I know it's not. But I can't . . ." Belladonna makes a frustrated sound. "I *hate* this. I hate that I know what I want and can't make myself reach out. I hate that I'm not even sure I believe in hell but I'm still scared of going there for wanting things that aren't a nice churchgoing husband and a life spent giving him obedience and children. I hate that I can hear *their* voices in my head."

Even as I tell myself to give her space, I can't resist stepping forward and gently drawing her into my arms. She doesn't hesitate to wrap her arms around me and hug me tight, her body shaking with the force of the conflict inside her. "If you want to talk about it, I'm here."

"I never fit," she whispers. "It started before I was born. My first memory is my mother telling me that the whole congregation knows I'm a sinful little beast and will do nothing but bring sorrow down on everyone I encounter."

"How old were you?"

"I don't remember exactly. Four or five."

Once again, murderous desire rises in me. I close my eyes and try to breathe through it, to keep my flames from betraying my rage. "You were a child. An innocent."

"No such thing according to our church." Her voice has gone a little watery. "Born with sin and all that. I made it to high school before I realized there was nothing I could do to earn their love. No matter how hard I tried, I would always be flawed in their eyes."

I swallow down the poisonous words I want to spit about her parents. "You mentioned a sister."

"I did." She sighs, slumping against me. "I love her so much. Ruth is a genuinely good person, but once I walked away from the church officially, it seemed like she had to *try* to love me back. It wasn't effortless or easy, and even when she said she loved me, there was an asterisk attached to it." Belladonna hiccups. "Hate the sin, love the sinner. But the so-called sin is *me*."

I stroke a hand down her long hair and hold her until her tremors ease. Only then do I guide her through the process of getting ready for sleep and tuck her into the massive four-poster bed. She looks young like this, innocent and scared. "I'm sorry, little one."

She swallows hard. "No, *I'm* sorry. I shouldn't have put this on you. You gave me a lovely night and I responded by weeping all over you."

I have to pause to make sure I can modulate the fierceness of my tone. "You have *nothing* to be sorry for. I will take your tears any day, Belladonna. They are as much a part of you as your laughter and your desire." I press a quick kiss to her forehead. "Sleep, little one." It's tempting to press a little magic behind that command, but I resist.

I don't go back to the party. I certainly don't go to bed. Instead, my footsteps trace the path to my study. As much as I'd like to spend my time out amongst my people, these days the true battles are fought through paperwork. Predatory trade agreements are just as threatening as a sword and offensive magic. Our territory isn't particularly rich in resources outside of lumber. We have small swaths of farmland, but only certain types of crops prosper here. We *need* trade with the dragons for wheat and the gargoyles for the medicinal herbs that grow in their mountains. Even with the krakens for the deepwater fish that could feed a small village for weeks. As for the bargainers, they deal in more elusive products, ferried back from other realms.

And none of them will commit to a long-term trade agreement between territories.

That leaves me begging for scraps from individual traders, most of whom are only too happy to raise their prices to predatory heights. Like the current asshole I'm engaging in a continued battle of letters with. He's a dragon who wants to pay half of fair market price for our lumber and for us to pay *double* for the wheat he has excess of.

I'm still hunched over my desk, cursing under my breath, when Danik steps through the door sometime later. His shirt is unbuttoned, and his eyes are heavy-lidded, but he seems alert enough as he drops into the chair across from my position behind the desk.

"You should be at the party," I say without looking up.

He raises his brows. "You either get me or you get all three of us. We had thought—hoped—Belladonna arriving in the territory might help you recover a little balance, but . . ." He waves a hand at my study. "Here you are, and there she is alone in her bed."

"She's been here a day," I snap.

"I know. Talk me through it. What's wrong?"

Damn it. I should have known that they noted my mood and decided to do something about it. I know what the proper thing to do is. Smile and make a joke, send him back to the revelry, continue my slow seduction of Belladonna, allow her to have a baby to benefit the territory and everyone who lives in it. That is the only course of action that will result in the outcome of what I've been working so hard for the last few years: to be a leader powerful enough to *make* the other territories pay attention, a fact that will be doubly true if Azazel has his way and finally puts us all on even territory.

I know that, and yet I can't banish the anger that roils inside me, sickening and so strong that it's no wonder the people who care most about me noticed. I grip the edge of my desk and barely resist the urge to sink my claws into the wood. "They *harmed* her. Her parents. Her community, if you can call it that. Even—maybe especially—the sister she sacrificed everything for."

"Yes."

I love him all the more for not arguing with me. "We can't kill them."

His voice is even and calm, a direct counterpoint to mine. "We don't have access to humans in the physical realm. We literally cannot kill them, morality arguments aside."

Which isn't to say we shouldn't. I study Danik, taking in the barely banked fury in his crimson eyes. "You're angry."

"Of course I am." He nods sharply. "Even though she's only been here a short time, we can tell she's a good girl,

sweet and kind. In the midst of your magic, even with
Zhenya boosting it with everything ze has, none of us
missed the soul wound Belladonna carries. She didn't
acquire that on her own."

No, she didn't. There are names behind that wound,
names of people still walking around, benefiting from *her*
sacrifice.

My claws prick the surface of the desk, and I make an
effort to raise my hands and place them on my thighs.
"Danik."

"I'm listening."

"Find them." I should feel guilt for this order. Succubi
and incubi may have a shitty reputation, but for generations
we have tried to feed ethically. There are plenty of willing
dreamers, happy to entangle themselves in our spells of lust
—more than enough for our entire population to gorge
nightly, even with the toll it takes us to reach across the
distance between realms.

"Find them," I repeat. It's on the tip of my tongue to
expand on that, to tell him that they aren't to get another
peaceful night's sleep. We can do that. We may prefer to feed
on lust and desire, but we can feed on fear all the same. It's
not as satisfying for anyone, but it *is* possible.

Frustration flares and I close my eyes, allowing the
emotion to slice through me. "Just . . . find them."

"Rusalka."

Reluctantly, I open my eyes. "What?"

Danik watches me closely. "I'm angry, too, but even
knowing Belladonna as short a time as we have, you must
know that she'd never agree to you hurting her parents—
even in their dreams. And doing so might violate her agreement with Azazel, which would potentially send her back to
that realm early."

I don't want to hear what he's saying. I *hate* that he's right. "Then what would you have me do?"

He's silent for long enough that my patience wears thing. Finally, Danik says, "Care for her. Allow her feel at home here. Give her the space to heal." A longer hesitation. "Maybe even allow her the opportunity to discover that true love comes without strings attached." He turns and walks away, calling softly over his shoulder. "In a year, if you still want me to find her parents, I will. But not before then."

13

BELLADONNA

After a dreamless sleep, I wake in the morning and lie in my bed for several long moments, staring at the ceiling. After what happened with Inna and the others, I'd expected the pleasure to extend past my waking moments. I'd . . . wanted to see Rusalka within the safety of dreams, to gather the courage to do the thing I couldn't quite manage in the daylight. To touch her.

Instinctive tension tries to fight its way into my muscles in response to that desire. I know what my mother would say—a whole host of ugly terms that I refuse to let my brain formulate on purpose—and I know what Pastor John and my father would say—*sin is tempting for a reason, so as to guide people off the straight and narrow*. I even know what Ruth would say, tears in her eyes—how she would beg me to pray with her as if this is a rotten part of me to be pruned away by faith.

But . . . even the weight of others' condemnation can't quite touch the golden dome around the memory. The pleasure, yes, but also the tenderness and care. I barely know Zhenya, Inna, and Danik, but I'd felt cherished all the same.

Which is not even getting into how protected and safe I feel with Rusalka, even when desire for her makes me dizzy.

This doesn't feel dirty. It doesn't feel *wrong*.

As I dress, I mull over what Rusalka told me about the god of the incubi and succubi, a great, unknowable being they worship through adhering to their nature because how could something intrinsic to your nature be a sin?

It's enough to make my head spin.

I pull on another dress, this one much more modest than last night's, and open the door to peek out. The hallway is empty, and I can't decide if I'm relieved or disappointed. In the end, it doesn't matter. I'm too hungry to hide in my bedroom until someone comes to fetch me.

From the little I've seen of the house, I can tell it's big but laid out in easy-to-navigate lines. After a little trial and error, I find a kitchen on the same side of the building as my bedroom but down on the first floor.

There's a person there who doesn't look like any incubus or succubus I've seen so far. Their skin is a deep-crimson color, and they have horns similar to Azazel's, though they're nowhere near his size. And they have a *second* set of horns growing out of where their eye sockets would be.

They turn to face me as I step through the door. "Belladonna, it's lovely to make your acquaintance. I'm here on behalf of Azazel, and I'll be doing periodic check-ins to ensure you're cared for and unharmed during your time in this territory."

The words have the flow of a rehearsed speech, are almost stilted. I edge farther into the kitchen and slide into a chair that allows me to see the whole of the room. "Rusalka has been above reproach as a host." My words are just as stilted as theirs, but I can't help that. I don't like the idea of *check-ins*. Azazel obviously doesn't trust me to know my own mind, and even if he's not trying to force me to act in a certain way, like my parents did, the very concept chafes.

"Of that I have no doubt." They grin, a sharp slash of white teeth and amusement. "I'm Ramanu, by the way. They/them."

Maybe I should find it strange that there are so many nonbinary people in this realm, but I suspect it's more a reflection of where I come from than where I've ended up. Back home is not exactly a welcoming environment for people who don't fit in the confined boxes prescribed by the church—gender, sexuality, and otherwise.

"It's nice to meet you," I say stiffly.

"No, it's not." They laugh, a musical sound that draws me in despite myself. "No one likes a babysitter, and territory leaders least of all. Rusalka is the best of the bunch, my own monarch excluded of course. Court loyalty and all that." They wave the concept away as if it doesn't matter. "Rusalka tells me that you've already decided to have a child to benefit the territory." They don't sound any happier with the information than anyone else has since I stated my intentions.

It's *irritating*. I cross my arms over my chest. "That *is* the purpose I was brought here to fulfill. I don't understand why everyone is getting so precious about someone agreeing to the very thing they want. I may not know Rusalka well, but even with the little I *do* know about them, I think there's no way they would force someone into that position. So . . ." I catch sight of their blatant effort not to laugh, and I glare. "Back off."

They chuckle under their breath. "With how Azazel and Rusalka are acting, I expected to find a quivering mess of a human, and yet here you are." They circle around the counter and set a plate of food in front of me. I can't quite define what the things on my plate are, but the smells are amazing. "You're no wilting flower, are you?"

I accept a fork and poke at what might be a root vegetable. "I understand my past trauma makes everyone nervous, but I'm more than capable of making my own decisions."

"So it would seem," Ramanu muses. They sink gracefully into the chair across from me and prop their elbows on the small table between us. I almost tell them to get their elbows off the table, but realize that's my mother talking, not me.

My first bite of the food has a surprised noise slipping free. I cover my mouth with my hand. "This is good."

"I'm a demon of many talents." They examine their claws, a deep black that looks similar to that of the incubi and succubi. "I do have one question, though."

I pause in the midst of taking a second bite. This feels like a trap. "Yes?"

"You're right. You show every evidence of being a smart person who is more than capable of making their own choices."

I wait. This must be a trap. They're being too nice to me. But then, hasn't *everyone* been too nice to me, from Azazel, with the initial contract, to every person I've come into contact with since? The deep suspicion in me comes from a lifetime of backhanded compliments and condemnations. "That's a statement."

"Indeed." Ramanu doesn't make me wait long. They push their chair back and rise. "My question is one I don't need an answer to—but *you* should answer it to yourself."

I set down my fork. "Are you normally this dramatic?"

"Always." They laugh. "Like I said, no one doubts your ability to make a decision. What I think you should examine closely from all angles is *why* you're making that decision."

An easy enough question to answer. "It helps people."

"Mmm." They turn away. I belatedly notice that they're wearing some kind of tunic with the sides split and what appear to be short shorts beneath it. They pause in the doorway. "And why do you want to help people so desperately, Belladonna? Is it out of genuine desire? Or is it because you don't think you have worth if you're not of use?" They slip out of the room before I can form an answer.

Even so, my jaw works and I sputter, "That's not why!" There's no answer, of course. True to their word, Ramanu doesn't seem to care what my answer is. And why should they? I'm doing what everyone wants. It's incredibly frustrating that no one seems happy about it. If I'd been able to do what my parents and pastor wanted, to fulfill their requirements as easily as I'm able to for Rusalka and her territory, my family would have been beside themselves with joy over what an obedient daughter I was. Instead, all I get are *questions*.

Or is it because you don't think you have worth if you're not of use?

I slump back in my chair. I have a feeling Ramanu's question is going to haunt me for a long, long time.

14

RUSALKA

The next few days fall into an uneasy rhythm. I don't want to push Belladonna, to *preach* to her. She's had enough of that in her life. Instead, I set about showing her around her new home. We meander through the shops in the square and then venture outward in slow spirals that take days. I show her how the homes and families are arranged: the most vulnerable of our population closer to the center, and those trained in defense closer to the edges. We haven't had war in a very long time, but there are other dangers. Hellcats, in particular—known to eat the unwary person—not to mention the other large predators that make their homes in the forests of my territory.

The community gardens delight her so much that she forgets her nerves and shame and quizzes the head gardener, Bogdan, about the plants until he huffs in surrender and tells her that if she's going to take up his time, the least she can do is help. I watch closely, ready to jump in if Belladonna wilts, but she just smiles and says, "Teach me. Please."

The next day, she's out there before I'm even up, dressed in pants and a tunic that she must have asked someone for, because I know they weren't among the items I ordered for her wardrobe. I wouldn't *know* she'd gone if I were working like I normally would be, holed up in my study. Right about now, I should be taking my coffee as I read through correspondence to figure out what needs to be responded to quickly and what can be left for a later hour.

Instead I'm on the west balcony of the manor, sipping my coffee and watching Belladonna and Bogdan in the garden. I can see most of the village from here, and though I can't pick up Belladonna's features at this distance, I can see that her body language is relaxed and easy. Even Bogdan has lost some of the customary tension he maintains; I've only ever seen him this patient when teaching the village children.

"She seems to be settling in."

"In some ways." I don't look over to where Inna leans against the balcony. My court has been checking up on me throughout each day, and they can't quite decide if they're worried or pleased. I'm not acting like myself.

Inna sighs. "I didn't really want to be the one to have this conversation with you, but we drew straws, so here I am."

That's enough to have me turning to give them my full attention. "That's a very serious statement for so early in the morning."

"I'm not going to tell you what do to with her, Rusalka." They shake their head. "And I'm not going to lecture you on all the risks and rewards. We both know you're already aware of them."

Tension coils along my spine. "It sounds like the only talk we're having is what you're *not* going to say."

"Don't get pissy." They prop their elbows on the railing.

"What I *am* going to say is that you should examine the awful feeling of watching someone you care about hurt themself for the greater good. Really wrap your hands around it, you know?"

This is leading somewhere and I don't like it. "Why?" I snap.

Inna turns and looks at me fully. "Because it's what we've been feeling for years, watching you drive yourself into the ground to protect us. You kill yourself just to make life a tiny bit better, to improve things for our people even a sliver." They hold up a hand before I can dredge up a response. "I'm not here to battle you about choices already made and actions already committed."

Some of the fight goes out of me. This is a conversation we've revisited over the years, usually when one of my court is scraping me off the ground after I've collapsed in exhaustion, metaphorically or otherwise, though that's only happened literally a few times. "Inna..."

"I like her, Rusalka. I don't want to see her hurt herself, even if it benefits us." Inna holds my gaze. "Just... think about the correlations, yeah?"

I swallow hard. "I will."

They nod slowly. "The week you demanded she take is almost up. What will you do if she doesn't change her mind?"

That question has kept me from sleep. Because Inna is right. How many times have I been faced with my decisions to help my people even at great personal cost to myself? How many times have I moved forward without care for the price? It's hypocritical in the extreme to keep Belladonna from doing the same.

But, gods, she's been through so much and has scars that go soul deep. "If I allow her to make this decision without any pushback, that will reinforce her belief that she's only worth what she can provide."

"Her belief that she's only worth what she can provide," Inna echoes slowly.

I take another sip of my coffee, a longer one this time. "I hear you, okay? I recognize the mirror being held up in front of me." Now, at least. "But I don't know what I'll do, Inna. That's the only answer I have."

Inna doesn't press further. I love them for that, even if I know it's their preferred way to operate—to lay out the facts and let the other person come to their own conclusions.

All too soon, my mug is empty and my excuse for hiding up here on this balcony is gone. Since taking over the leadership role, I've never once avoided work that needed to be done until now. But Belladonna feels like a magnet, drawing me toward her despite myself. Not that I'm trying to avoid it all that much.

Even so, I can't avoid my responsibilities any longer. I sigh. "Can you keep an eye on her? I don't expect she'll come to any harm in the gardens or the village, but—"

"You worry." Inna squeezes my shoulder. "I understand. It's been a while since I've worked a shift in the gardens. Bogdan will be content enough with the extra set of hands."

"Thank you." Some of the tightness leaves my shoulders. "I appreciate it."

"I like her." Inna takes my mug and turns toward the door, a clear order to stop moping and get back to the many tasks that come with leadership. "We all do."

Historically, I've found peace in the minutiae of paperwork. Peoples don't sing ballads about the wars that are fought and won over contracts and trading agreements, but I've been bloodied in wars immortalized in songs and I'd rather the backache from hunching over my desk for hours on end. If I do my job right, no one has to die.

At my desk is where Belladonna finds me, hours and hours later, when the sun hangs low in the sky outside the large windows in my study. She slips through the door with her head bent low, as if she expects to be yelled at for intruding. I know it's a learned behavior, so as much as it stings to see, I don't mention it. Hopefully one day she'll feel safe enough here that some of her tension eases, but that's not something that can be rushed.

"Am I interrupting?"

I smile and stretch, several bones in my spine popping loudly. "Saving me, more like." I survey her, taking in how her hair has gone frizzy with the humidity and her cheeks still have a deep glow from spending time outside. There's a smudge of dirt on her brow and more marking her clothes. She looks . . . happy. "The gardens are well?"

"Yes." She smiles, and it's the first sunrise after a vicious storm, filled with hope and the promise of more. "It's so lovely. Bogdan has taught me so much, and I'm getting better at telling weeds from proper plants. Later this week, he's going to show me the vegetables and fruits that need to be replanted each year and how he cycles through them to ensure the soil remains healthy."

Her happiness buoys me out of my chair and guides me around the desk until I stand before her. "It sounds like you're enjoying yourself."

"Yes." It's almost more sigh than word. She looks so damned kissable that I have to clench my fists to avoid reaching for her. Belladonna smiles sweetly. "Bogdan is gruff, but he's not cruel. It's comforting now that I've gotten used to him."

Even as I tell myself not to move, to be patient, to let her come to me, my body isn't listening. I find myself stroking my claws across her cheek. To my surprise, she leans into the touch and closes her eyes. "I'm glad you've found something you enjoy," I say softly, not wanting to shatter the moment. "Spend as much time there as you want."

"Just like that?"

"Just like that. Everyone chooses their role in this territory. There are jobs no one particularly wants that we require everyone to cycle through for a short time, but other than that, they follow their joy." I twine a strand of her hair around my finger and slowly draw it out before letting it fall back to her shoulder.

Belladonna's eyes shine in a worrisome way, but she's smiling. "I know I've said I don't believe in hell, which means I probably shouldn't believe in heaven, but when I *did* believe, this is kind of what I always imagined heaven to be like."

I shake my head. "This is real life, little one. There are occasionally challenges with doing things this way. They're usually easily surmountable, but the fact remains that the challenges exist."

I don't know what I expect her to say in response to that, but she licks her lips. "I want to kiss you."

The moment feels unreal. I haven't been nervous about kissing someone since I was young, awkward, and filled with more need than I knew how to satisfy. That was years and years ago, and yet my hands shake as I slowly cup Belladonna's hips. "I want you to kiss me." I tug her closer. "Please."

She slowly mirrors my position, taking my hips. It's a little awkward but somehow sexier for it. Then she goes up onto her tiptoes and kisses me. It's a light sensation, a faint brushing of her lips to mine, a sweet touch that seduces me right down to my soul.

It wasn't supposed to be like this. From the moment I agreed to Azazel's deal, I intended to care for my chosen human, to ensure she was protected and her every need was seen to. But I didn't expect to *feel* all these ways. Protective and needy and so fucking angry. I want to slice her family to pieces, to burn their damned church to the ground, maybe to burn *every* church to the ground to save the future Belladonnas of her realm. This fury is not me, but as she sighs into my mouth, I'm having a hard time remembering why I *can't* do all that, beyond the logistics of not being able to travel to the human realm.

All the while, I hold her gently. I allow her to explore my lips, then finally part them and let her inside when it becomes clear she doesn't know how to ask. Even then, I keep the majority of my desire chained and choked. The kiss grows, warm and slick and needy—and *us*. No magic paves the way to her submission.

She leans in, or maybe I tug her closer, and then she's pressed to my body, her softness a temptation I want to explore with my tongue. I stumble back, taking her with me, to sit on the edge of the desk. I'm tall enough that she ends up straddling my thigh.

Belladonna gasps so sweetly at the contact to her pussy through her pants. That should be enough to shock me back to my senses, but the spell of desire is too strong. I slip my hand around to cup the base of her skull. Desire, we've had in abundance. This feels deeper, stronger. *Need* doesn't begin to cover it.

She loops her arms around my neck and gives herself over to me completely. The trust nearly sends me to the floor. It chains me all the tighter. I am filled with as much conflict as Belladonna carries inside her daily.

Go gently.

The reminder is what I needed in order to snap me back into the moment, away from the fear of misstepping. I stroke my hands down her back to cup her hips. Her kiss goes frantic for the first time as I guide her to roll her hips and rub herself against my thigh. Desperate. Needy. Begging for more.

I have more to give.

15

BELLADONNA

I've wanted to kiss Rusalka for *days*. Maybe from the moment I met her. I don't know. I can't *think* when she's kissing me like this, like she has all the time in the world, like she wants to memorize my taste, like maybe she actually cares about me for more than what I'm able to give her. The thought boggles my mind.

Or maybe it's the slow friction against her thigh that's boggling my mind and scattering my thoughts. My whole body lights up with the contact. She seems to know it, though I can't begin to guess if it's due to her succubus powers or simply instinct. Rusalka always seems to know what I need.

My panties are slick with my need, which adds to the grinding desire that sparks through my veins. Again and again.

Rusalka keeps one hand at my hip and bends me back a little so they can kiss down my jawline to my throat. They drag their tongue over my pulse as if they can taste it beneath my skin. "Come for me, little one."

My brain blanks. I try to wrest control back, to frantically grind at their leg, but Rusalka holds me steady, forcing me to keep the rhythm slow.

She chuckles. "Slow, Belladonna. Some things can't be rushed."

I don't understand that. The only times I dared touch myself in the dark of the night were frantic guilt-ridden experiences that I simultaneously craved and wanted over as quickly as possible. Even after I left the church and became determined to go my own way, I couldn't shake the shameful feelings when stroking myself to completion.

She doesn't let me lead, and somehow that unblocks something in my brain. I don't have to fight this. I can simply allow the river of lust to take me and trust Rusalka to care for me.

As soon as the thought fades, my body takes over. The hot knot of need in my core explodes. "*Rusalka*," I sob out. "Oh . . . my . . . I . . ." I keep speaking, but the words lose any meaning.

They keep my hips rolling for a few more beats and then ease me back to slump against them. They rub slow circles on my back as I learn how to breathe for what feels like the first time. I try to tense, prepared for the wave of shame that always comes after anything sex related, even if it only happens in my head. The shame is there. I can feel it waiting in the wings. But it can't touch me right now, not as I'm safely encircled in Rusalka's arms.

I bury my face in their throat and hug them tightly, wanting this moment to last forever. It's only as my heartbeat slowly returns to normal that I realize how selfish I've been. I try to lift my head, but Rusalka catches me. "What brings that tension into your body, Belladonna?" they ask carefully.

It strikes me that they've been careful with me from the

beginning. Maybe I could learn a thing or two from that. I swallow hard. "You didn't ... I didn't ..."

She laughs softly. Kindly. "This isn't tit for tat, little one. I don't require an orgasm just because I gave you one. Your pleasure is enough for now."

I want to keep arguing, but Ramanu's question circles in my head, stalling me. Am I pushing this because I want to or out of obligation? Even as I wonder, I know the truth. I *crave* to see Rusalka undone in the same way that they undid me. "I want to."

Their hand pauses its tracing of soothing circles on my back. "Next time, little one."

I open my eyes, not sure when I closed them. "Do you ... not want me to?"

She freezes. "That's not what I said."

"But you're brushing me off. If you don't want to, it's okay. I don't want you to feel obligated, contract or no." I don't lift my head from her shoulder. I'm not brave enough to look into her face as I say this. "But if you want me as much as you seem to ... Rusalka, I want you, too." She didn't use magic on me this time. My thoughts are clear, remarkably so.

I slip out of her arms to kneel at her feet. Rusalka looks taller like this, towering over me in all her perfection. Her tail flicks next to me, but I don't understand succubi enough to know if it's in agitation or something else.

I carefully place my hands on her thighs. "Please, Rusalka." I lick my lips, want making me lightheaded. "I don't really know what I'm doing, but you could show me. I want to. I really, really want to."

For a long moment, I think she might reiterate her rejection. Instead she worries at her bottom lip. "I don't want to be another memory that you flog yourself with at the altar of your cruel god."

I flinch. I can't help it. They're right, even if I'm fighting against doing exactly that. "I'm a work in progress. I'm trying to learn to reach for what I want. For . . . who . . . I want."

Her exhale is loud between us. Finally she nods. "If you're sure."

"I am." I fumble at the front of her pants until she nudges my hands away and undoes them herself. A few quick jerks and they're on the floor and . . .

Rusalka is as beautiful here as everywhere else. I got a good look at Zhenya the other night, and zir anatomy seemed similar to a human's, at least to mine, but Rusalka is shaved except for a strip of hair above her . . . pussy. Almost like a direction, an invitation.

I shift closer, between their thighs, and try to remember what Inna did to me. It seems to me that sex is like any other skill and there's a wide spectrum of experience, but thinking about it like that only reinforces how little I know what I'm doing. Sex with Jacob was a submission, a flurry of lust and shame and unfulfilled need. This is different in so many ways.

Wrong, that ugly voice inside me whispers.

I shove it away and dive into Rusalka. The shame stays away when I'm too busy *feeling*, so I'll never stop feeling. Especially when the first drag of my tongue through their folds makes Rusalka moan. Just a little, but that's enough to incite me further.

More than that, they taste . . . It's so different than I expected when I dared imagine what being with someone who has a similar body to mine would be like. Salty and something unidentifiable, something *good*. I want more.

Rusalka shifts and spreads their legs wider. "Take your time, little one." Their voice is breathy, but still controlled.

The permission is exactly what I need. I lick and taste and occasionally nibble, exploring them even as I pay attention to what touches and pressure makes their breathing change. I've spent my entire life watching those around me and adjusting my actions and words in response. I've never done it like *this*, with only pleasure in mind.

It feels like liberation.

A brush between my thighs startles me. I look down to find Rusalka's tail. *"Oh."*

"Take off your pants, Belladonna." Their voice has gone low and sensual. It doesn't feel the way their magic did the other night, but it weaves a spell around me all the same. I awkwardly wrestle out of my pants and kick them away. Within seconds, I'm rewarded by that tufted tail pressing to my pussy through my soaked panties. I whimper, and Rusalka laces their claws through my hair. "I love how wet I make you."

"I love how wet *I* make *you*." The words feel just as sinful on my tongue as her taste, and yet for the first time, that's a thrill instead of a shame. I look up her perfect body. "Show me how to make you orgasm. Please."

They smile, the expression somehow both caring and lustful. I didn't know those two things could go hand in hand. They tug me gently up to their clitoris. "Right here, little one. Slow strokes with the flat of your tongue." As I obey, eager to feel them come all over my face, they start rolling their hips in a rhythm identical to that of their tail rubbing against my pussy. Pleasure surges, driving me before it. I'm going to come again, but I refuse to let it happen without Rusalka there beside me.

I'm so busy fighting to give her exactly what she asked

for that at first I don't notice the buzzing against my tongue. How could I? My entire body is buzzing at this point. But with each stroke, it gets stronger, and I belatedly realize that her clitoris is *vibrating*.

I force my eyes open and watch her head fall back as pleasure takes her, as pleasure takes us both. At the same time, flames erupt at her back and form a familiar shape that almost shocks me into freezing. *Wings*.

When Rusalka orgasms, she looks like an angel.

16

RUSALKA

I don't mean to end up on the floor, but my knees won't quite hold me after that orgasm. I lean against my desk and tuck Belladonna under my arm. She melts against me. It feels so damned *right* that I'm unprepared for the shame that rolls in like a tsunami.

Belladonna starts to shake. "I'm sorry."

Once again, I have to forcibly remind myself that I can't kill her entire family for putting these scars on her. Even if it were possible, were to feel good in the moment, it wouldn't change the past. The scars they put on Belladonna have to heal on their own. But I'll be damned before I let them get access to her in the future.

I keep my touch gentle as I stroke her shoulder. If she feels cornered, that'll pull harder on all the things she's trying to move past. "You should stay."

She lifts her head. "What?"

I didn't mean to offer, but I'm not about to walk it back. "Here. In this realm, in my territory. You should stay. Even after the seven years have expired."

Her eyes go big. "That's . . ." She swallows hard. "That's an option?"

"Yes. If you want it to be." I press a light kiss to her forehead and rise, tugging her to her feet. "It's your choice, Belladonna. It's always been your choice. My people adore you."

"They don't know me. I've only been here a week." She looks away and slips her hand from mine. "Eventually I'll disappoint them."

"None of that." Maybe I should let her retreat, but I can't quite manage to. I catch her chin lightly and turn her face back to mine. "We all disappoint people sometimes. It's part of life. That doesn't mean you don't deserve peace."

"Peace." Her gaze goes distant before refocusing on me with new intentness. "You'd let me stay."

"Yes. Regardless of whether you decide to go through with a pregnancy. Regardless of anything. Bogdan will need to take an apprentice soon; he's been putting it off for years, but he likes you. Or, if the gardens don't interest you, there are many other options."

She's looking at me as if she's never seen me before. "You really mean that. All of it."

"Yes." There's no other answer. It's the truth.

"What happens if we keep doing this?" She waves vaguely around us, where sex still hangs heavy in the air. "What happens if it goes badly? You won't want to see me around. What if we do this, and we have a child, and then it doesn't work out?"

Ah. I could tell her that I've never done this before. I've had lovers and partners, many of whom are still friends, but anytime the connection with one of those people threatened to distract me from my responsibilities, I ended things. The happiness I felt with them was too selfish to allow to continue. My people needed me, and *they* were worth any amount of heartbreak I experienced personally. It always hurt, but ultimately it was an easy choice to make.

It feels different with Belladonna. I've never felt the ground crumbling beneath my feet and experienced exhilaration instead of fear. I've never wanted to wrap up a lover and protect them from everything—including the sacrifices required to benefit the whole of my territory. Until now.

Admitting as much will panic her. It might even put pressure on this thing that isn't even a thing, not quite. "I am leader of this territory, and I will continue to put the good of the territory before any personal feelings. I can't imagine it becoming an issue, but if for some reason I couldn't perform my duties fairly, I'd step down." I take a deep breath, not prepared to deal with the surge of feelings that comes from the idea of a child of mine and Belladonna's. "Obviously a child would complicate things, but that possible future is still far away. I don't want to make decisions based on fear, little one. I want to make them with hope in my heart."

"You can't step down." She stumbles back a step. "Not because of me."

"I have no intention of it becoming an issue." This conversation has already gotten too tangled. She's only been here a week, and she already has me twisted up in knots. I don't know how any of us will survive seven years, let alone longer. "Come on. I'll see you to your bedroom."

She's silent up the stairs and down the hall, but as we reach her door, Belladonna digs in her heels. "You have to know how abnormal it is for things to be this easy, this good. Surely you can understand why it feels like a trap?"

Her words hurt, little cuts that make me bleed. I refuse to show it. It's not her fault. "What is normal, Belladonna?"

She opens her mouth, but I press forward.

"Is it guilt and shame poured onto the shoulders of the young, a thousand instances of telling them that that they're flawed and dirty and wrong?" I shake my head. "That's not my normal. It never will be. I understand that this is a large change for you—for both of us—and it's difficult to process, but what you feel over natural desires is not *normal*—if such a thing even exists."

Her mouth works, and I almost leave without waiting for her to find her words. But that would be cruel and selfish in its own right. She slumps back against the door frame, then finally speaks. "You're right. I'm sorry."

"Stop apologizing." I take a breath and try to temper the sharpness of my tone. "Please."

"It's proper to apologize when one is wrong," she says tartly, but the sass fades immediately. "How does your god feel about shame and guilt?"

I shrug. "I don't have an easy answer for you, little one. Those emotions are part of life. It's only when they take over and unbalance everything that it's a problem. We don't have a set of rules to follow. We use our instincts. Worship and faith look a little different for each individual."

"I don't understand that," she whispers. "I'm trying to, but it's so hard to unlearn things that were drilled into my head as fact for so long."

"Give yourself grace. It's only been a week."

She shifts from foot to foot. "Rusalka?"

"Yes?"

Belladonna opens the door and steps into her room. "Would you like to come in?" She must see the polite refusal in my face, because she straightens her shoulders. "Would you like to come in and stay? The night. Naked, preferably. If you want to."

I blink. Of all the things I anticipated her saying, this

wasn't on the list. I tentatively taste her emotions, half-sure that she's using me to flog herself, but her shame is a dull undertone compared to her bright desire. Her feelings aren't purely lust either. She . . . cares.

She cares, and she's reaching out in tentative faith. Even if I didn't want her desperately, I wouldn't refuse her this. "Are you sure?"

"Yes." Her gaze flicks to my shoulders as if she can still see the fire that appears when I lose control. "Will it burn me?"

"No. It's not that kind of fire." My fire *can* be a weapon in battle, but it takes conscious effort and it's incredibly draining. In bed play, using it is as natural as breathing, same as the incubi's shadows. An extension of self. I clear my throat. "You don't have to sleep with me in order to stay here, little one. I'm not monster enough to require that. It's the antithesis of everything we are."

She smiles, sweet and a little pleased. "I know." She steps back, and her hands go tentatively to the hem of her shirt. "I want you, Rusalka. I want you so desperately, it's like a fever in my blood. Even when I'm up to my elbows in dirt in the garden, you're all I can think about."

I follow her into the room and shut the door, but I still hesitate to close the distance between us. Foolish, maybe, considering the orgasms I teased out of her just a short time ago, considering the fact that I can still scent myself on her lips. But then, I've been foolish when it comes to this woman from the moment we met. "I don't want to inadvertently harm you by moving too fast."

Her lower lip quivers, and she makes a visible effort to still it. "It's because you care so much that I want this. Because you're *you*. I had fun with Zhenya, Inna, and Danik, but they aren't *you*. If I just wanted sex, I would find someone else, but that's not what I want."

The last of my resistance fades away. How could it do anything else when she's standing before me, so fucking brave that it takes my breath away? "I care about you, too."

"I know." Belladonna smiles, and some of the tension fades away. "I know," she repeats.

"If at any point, you change your mind, this stops with no negative consequences. Whether that's tonight or three weeks or three years from now." I reach out slowly and lace my fingers through hers. "Never doubt that you're safe with me."

"I know I am." She laughs, the sound kind of tentative but true. "Rusalka, please take off your clothes."

Now it's my turn to laugh. "No, little one. If you want me in your bed, then we're going to do this properly."

"*Is* there a proper way to do it?"

I guide her through the room toward the bathroom. "If by 'it,' you're referring to sex, then no, there's no specific way that qualifies as proper. But we're not talking about sex."

"We're . . . not?"

I nudge her onto the stool next to the bath and turn on the water. "No, dear heart. You said you want to take me to bed. That's seduction." That's *caring*, with the potential for something deeper. Every interaction I've had with Belladonna reinforces the truth that she's never been able to grasp the idea of sex as something free from shame, something that doesn't have to be hurried and guilt-ridden. "We have all night, and I intend to use every minute to its fullest."

17

BELLADONNA

I t takes only a few minutes to get the tub filled. Rusalka won't allow me to undress myself, and I understand why the moment she slides her hands up my sides and guides my shirt over my head.

There's seduction even in this. It's there in the way their breath ghosts over my shoulder, a tease at a future kiss, in how their claws play along my stomach before carefully undoing my pants, in the stroke of their tail up my calf, over my knee, to my inner thigh. The touches aren't overtly sexual, but they're filled with tenderness and *caring*. They make my knees go weak.

Still, I catch their hand and lift it to press a kiss to their palm. "I want you to touch me everywhere, but I have to admit I'm nervous about your claws."

Rusalka's laugh rumbles through her chest and into mine. "Have faith, little one. As I mentioned before, my people are shape-shifters." She tugs her hand from mine and holds it up in front of my face. There's a faint shimmer, the promise of flames, and then her claws melt down to mostly human-looking fingers. They're too long, an extra knuckle in the place of the sharp claw. A pulse of heat goes through me and centers right between my thighs.

"Oh," I say faintly.

They finish undressing me and urge me into the bath. "You worked hard in the gardens today. I imagine you're feeling it."

Truth be told, I am. I've had a job of one kind or another since I was sixteen, but none of them involved much manual labor. I didn't expect to find such peace in it. Neither did I expect to find such satisfaction in the gardens itself. In knowing that when the seasons turn and turn again, I'll plant and nurture and harvest a bounty that will feed not only myself but this community. A community that seems to have welcomed me with open arms. Knowing that is more than worth the aching back and the cramping fingers and the dirt that seems determined to work itself into every nook and cranny of my skin. "I like it."

"I can tell." They urge me down until I'm submerged up to my chin. "Let the hot water start the process of unwinding those tight muscles, and I'll take care of the rest. Give me your hand."

Even though I try to focus, to watch her, my eyes slide shut as she takes a small brush and goes to work on the dirt embedded in my nail beds. The bath and the pampering feel divine. "You aren't trying to soothe me to sleep so you don't have to come to bed with me, are you?"

Rusalka's low laugh makes me open my eyes. Their full lips are pulled in a wicked grin that chases the thought of sleep right from my head. "I'm merely giving you a moment of rest. Enjoy it."

As if I can do anything else. The heat works into my muscles, then my bones, and Rusalka's hands do the rest. She washes me. It's an act that should probably feel wrong or make humiliation lash my skin, but with Rusalka, it's as natural as breathing. I trust her implicitly.

Maybe that makes me a fool. Only time will tell. If they really want to take advantage of me, it will be easy enough. I've given them the lock, the keys, and everything that I am. They wouldn't even have to work hard at manipulation. They'd merely need to tell me again that my sacrifice would benefit thousands upon thousands of people.

My head lolls on the edge of the tub as they wash my hair. The weight of my tresses is heavy, and, not for the first time, I think about cutting it. I'm not even sure I *like* long hair; it's simply been the only option available to me.

Just like that, I've made a decision. "I want to cut my hair."

Their hands are still in the middle of massaging my scalp. "You do?"

"Yes." It's the truth. It's never been truer.

To Rusalka's credit, they don't ask me if I'm sure. "How short?"

I start to sit up. "Do you have a knife?"

She grabs my shoulders, keeping me in place. "Let's make one thing clear, little one. Under no circumstances am I going to hand you a knife and let you hack your own hair off. Tell me how short you would like it, and I'll cut it for you."

I twist just enough to see her, to see how serious she is. Another type of care. My heart thumps almost painfully in my chest. "Above my shoulders."

"After your bath." They finish washing my hair, their claws once again in evidence and gently massaging my scalp. It almost works to fade the tension of anticipation making me quiver. Rusalka knows. Of course they know.

In no time, they get me out of the bath and dry me with

a large fluffy towel, ignoring my insistence that I can dry myself. I wait for shame to take me in response to my being naked in front of another person without even having the decency to wait for the deepest night. But it's hard to feel bad when Rusalka is so intent.

They pull out a robe from somewhere and dress me in it. Then they urge me into a chair that I hadn't noticed before. "Inna is quite good with hair, so they'll have to clean up this cut tomorrow. But I can manage to get the weight off your shoulders. Will that work?"

"Yes." She could have told me to wait for Inna to do it right. She could have handed me a knife and let me hack it off myself. She could have done a lot of things, but instead she's carefully sectioning my hair and running her fingers through it.

I don't understand exactly what she's doing until she stops, her fingers a few inches over my shoulder. "This length?"

I don't care about the specifics, but I suspect they don't want to hear that. "Yes," I say hoarsely. "That length."

Rusalka uses their claws to cut my hair in quick, efficient movements. It feels as though it should take longer, but within ten minutes or so, they run their fingers through my hair again. It's only when they urge me to the mirror near the sink that I realize they were drying my hair and that the heat I felt wasn't solely from their skin. They come to stand behind me, expression carefully gentle. "What do you think?"

I touch my hair gingerly. It's got so much more volume like this, bouncing above my shoulders with every movement. It feels like . . . freedom. "I love it."

"Good."

I keep staring at myself in the mirror. The length of my

hair is the only thing that's changed, and yet that's not the truth, is it? *Everything* has changed. Isn't it time I embraced that change fully? Before doubt can seep in, I turn and take Rusalka's hand. They allow me to lead them back into the bedroom and to the bed. "I don't want to wait anymore."

She opens her mouth like she might argue but pauses and studies my expression. "Just remember that you can stop this at any moment, regardless of what's happening."

"Rusalka." I wait for them to look at me. "I trust you. I want this. I promise I'll communicate if anything doesn't work for me."

They smile slowly and curl their fingers through mine. "Then *I'll* trust *you* to be honest with me."

"I will. I promise." I take another step toward the bed. "Please, Rusalka. I'm relaxed and seduced, and I need you right now."

Their smile gains the wicked edge I'm quickly learning to crave. "Oh, little one, there will be nothing rushed about this." They step closer, guiding me back onto the bed, then follow me down. Rusalka is already athletic and taller than me, but with their body pressing mine into the mattress, they feel so much . . . more. I don't know how to explain it; I only know that it makes me go soft and melty.

They brush my hair back from my face, spreading it out over the pillow, their amber eyes hot enough to truly melt me. "You please me so greatly."

My heart thumps so hard, it's a wonder they can't see it trying to beat itself out of my chest. I lick my lips. "I haven't done anything yet."

"You've done everything." She brushes a light kiss to my brow, my cheekbone, my jaw. "You're so selfless and kind. Curious and brave. Able to have your worldview challenged without it crushing you." She strokes her hand down to my hip and presses me harder to the mattress. "Smart. Strong. Beautiful."

I almost tell them that they don't have to lie to me, but I manage to stop the words before giving them voice. Rusalka's praise makes me uncomfortable in the way being perceived always has, but that doesn't mean they're lying. It doesn't mean they're wrong.

She doesn't give me time to think too hard. She kisses me. I thought the lead-up to getting into bed was a seduction. I'm a fool. This kiss is a thousand times more seductive. It starts off slow and almost tentative, a leisurely exploration of my lips. Then she teases my mouth open and *kisses* me.

I don't mean to move. One moment I'm gripping their biceps, and the next my hands are in their short hair and I'm trying to wrap one leg around their hips. Rusalka tenses their hand, keeping my hips pinned to the bed despite my writhing. It creates the tiniest distance between us. Too much. I hate it.

I break the kiss enough to gasp, "*More*."

18

RUSALKA

Belladonna takes to desire as if she were one of mine —born to it. She kisses me eagerly, her body already rising to meet mine. I slowly ease the kiss, pause to nip her bottom lip, and raise my head. "I have a question, and I want you to answer it honestly."

She blinks. "Okay."

"I'm going to spend the night worshipping your body with my mouth and fingers." My hands actually shake where I grip her hip. I don't try to fight the response. She deserves to know exactly how intensely she affects me.

"That . . . wasn't a question."

I laugh softly. "No, it wasn't. And it's actually two questions." I slide my thigh between hers. "Are you going to be a good girl and take your pleasure . . . or do I have to tie you down?"

Her eyes get wide. Her mouth works, but no sound comes out. I wait, giving her time to process . . . but not too much time. Thankfully, she manages to win whatever internal battle my words brought forth within a few beats.

"Tie me down." The words come out in a rush. "Tie me down so I can't stop you."

I shake my head. "You *can* stop me, with a single word." I enjoy games of protest when the mood strikes, but games have rules that must be abided by, and there's no way we're going *there* the first time I have her properly in her bed. Not when we haven't had a clearheaded negotiation ahead of time. "If you want to pretend I'm forcing you, that's something we can discuss—another night."

Belladonna sucks in a breath. "I don't . . ." She shakes her head. "I don't think I want *that*. That's not what I meant." I wait as she shifts beneath me, obviously uncomfortable with this frank discussion, but I'm not about to let her off the hook. Finally, she closes her eyes. "I meant that, even now, *their* voices are in the back of my mind, screaming that this is a sin. You tying me down isn't forcing me to do anything, and I don't want it to be. But it sounds like peace, and I want that."

That, I understand. Zhenya loves bondage. It's the only time ze calms down and goes all sleepy in a sexy sort of way. Still, I want to negotiate this carefully. No normal ropes will do for Belladonna. Not tonight. "If you like this, we'll try something more challenging to get out of another time. Put your hands over your head."

Belladonna tenses as if she'll argue with me, but she finally obeys, sliding her arms over her head. Her fingertips barely brush the headboard. I concentrate, drawing my fire and arranging it around her wrists. She gasps, and I glance down at her face. "Does it hurt?"

"No." She wiggles her fingers. "No, it's just warm pressure. It feels good."

Perfect. "You can break this binding easily. Lift your hands."

She obeys, hissing out a breath when her wrists easily slide through the flames. Not bondage, not properly, but a mindfuck that I think we're both going to get off on. I slide my hands over her arms, urging them back into place. "You're not really being held down. But you're not going to break these bonds, are you, little one? You're going to be good and obedient and accept the pleasure I give you."

"Y-yes." She licks her lips and squirms. "You said two questions."

Eager little thing. I love it. "I did, didn't I?" I form more flames around my fingers. "I said I would please you with my tongue and fingers, but I have an additional way if you're interested and willing."

"*Yes.*"

That draws a light laugh from me. "I haven't even told you what it is."

"It's you. Everything you do feels good to me." She holds my gaze. "Yes, Rusalka."

Her trust humbles me in a way that makes my throat threaten to close. I could press forward with these negotiations, but she's just as impatient as I am to move forward. I shift back to kneel between her thighs. The robe is oversized and only offers little slices of skin to entice—the grace of her wrists, the soft curve of the top of one breast, her pretty knees.

Knees. I truly am gone for this woman.

It's a nice robe. But having her naked will be even nicer. I lean forward, bracing myself on one hand above her, and trail a single finger over the robe. It takes concentration to ensure ramp up the fire to the point of burning, to demolish her robe, inch by inch, revealing her pink nipples, her soft stomach, her perfect pussy. All the better, she's shaking and panting by the time I'm done.

I tease my fire over her nipples, pulsing it softly until she moans. It can be as solid as I need, but for now, I want the suggestion of touch more than actual touch. Silly to be jealous of a fire that's my construction, but I have Belladonna naked and panting for the pleasure I intend to give her. I don't want to miss a moment.

Her nipples are warm and sweet against my tongue, her moans in response even sweeter. I tease one nipple to a tight point, then the other. All the while, I watch her face, read her desires. Both scream *more*, so more is what I give her. I keep my flames playing at her breasts and give them a little more weight to lift and stroke and tease as I shift down her body. Her skin is decadently soft and breaks out in goose bumps in the wake of my tongue. Gods, she's perfect, from her little moans to the stretch marks decorating her hips and stomach.

As if in response to my thought, her eyes fly open and she shifts. I pause, my breath ghosting over the skin below her belly button, and wait. "Problem?"

"No. Yes. I don't . . ." She closes her eyes and inhales deeply. "I'm self-conscious. I don't want you to think less of me for how I look."

I'm glad she has her eyes shut so she can't see the murderous urge rising in me again. It would put a damper on the mood. I have to bank it and bank it hard. "Would you like me to tell you what I see?"

"I don't know." She still has her eyes closed. "I might die of embarrassment if you do."

"Will you start disassociating if I don't?"

Belladonna finally looks at me. "You're too smart. It's uncomfortable to be seen like this."

I laugh even though my chest is tight. People are people, and we all have our little fracture points. Some are more pronounced than others, but all are worthy of care. "Do you want to stop?"

"No. Absolutely not." She shakes her head sharply. "You can . . ." She sucks in a harsh breath. "You can tell me what you see. I'll try not to hate it."

My laugh is a little too dry, but I can do this for her. I can make it good for her. And I'll be damned if she's not going to enjoy hearing it. I dip down and drag my tongue through her folds, earning a yip of surprise. That yip turns into a moan when I press a single finger into her warm, wet heat. "Gods, you are perfect."

"Rusalka . . .*Please*. You don't have to—"

I pump slowly, exploring her even as I keep a close eye on her face. "I mean it. You look at your body, at your soul, and see all the imperfections, not realizing that those imperfections add up to *you*, to Belladonna." I curl my finger against her inner wall and am rewarded by a sweet moan. Good. She's still fighting not to hear, even as she submits, her arms still stretched above her head, encircled by my fire. I kiss her lightly and work another finger into her. "Would you like to know a secret, little one?"

"Y-yes." She lifts her hips to guide my fingers deeper as her mouth seeks mine. "Please. Tell me."

Good girl. The trust she puts in me to take care of her, both physically and emotionally, is staggering. I've been taking care of my entire territory for most of my adult life, and yet this feels different. I would never call being a leader a burden—or not *just* a burden, because there is joy in seeing my people prosper and knowing it's, in part, because of my choices. But this? Belladonna? She's a damned *gift*. Battered and bruised and still striving forward without hesitation. Those bastards she calls family didn't break her. They didn't even get close.

I nip her bottom lip. "What your world calls perfection is boring. It's the so-called flaws that make us who we are." I press the heel of my hand to her clit even as I keep working that lovely little spot inside her. "It's the flaws and the bumps and bruises that make you perfect, little one. You're stronger for them, and *that* is true perfection."

"Rusalka," she gasps. "I can't. I'm so—"

"I've got you, little one." I don't stop. This is the first of many orgasms, and we both need it too much to stop. "Let go."

When she comes, it's with my name on her lips. Again. I slide down her body to settle between her thighs. It's a good thing she's interested in staying here permanently, because even after a week, she's shaken things down to their very foundations. She's shaken *me*.

I want to keep her.

19

BELLADONNA

I didn't know sex could be like this.

It's a thought I've had more than once since coming to this realm. It's intense and overwhelming, but there's joy as well. There's . . . fun. The delight is there in her low laugh when I push her onto her back and set about exploring her body as thoroughly as she explored mine. It's there in my glee at making her wings erupt from her back and her clitoris start vibrating from stroking her pussy with my tongue. Everything feels good and nothing feels bad, and I didn't know it could be like this.

Even outside of my ill-fated personal experience, some things were just *known*. Sex was something to be endured by women, something done to fulfill your role as a wife and, eventually, mother. Daring to want it with someone who isn't your husband, isn't a man at all? Unthinkable.

But, for the first time in my conscious life, there's barely any thought of *sin* as I lust, Rusalka sitting up and claiming my mouth, tasting herself there just as I taste myself on her tongue. She tugs me down onto her chest, ignoring my half-hearted protest about crushing her, and gathers me close. I only manage to tense for a few moments before relaxing against her.

"I'll stay."

They pause their stroking down my spine. "You don't have to give me an answer now. Or tomorrow. Or in the next few years. You've been pressured and cornered and pushed your entire life. I won't add to that."

I think I love you.

I know better than to say the words aloud. It's too soon for that sort of talk. And more likely, they would tell me that I'm only responding to the first kind and caring person I've ever met—maybe add a dose of *bonding over trauma* talk in the process. Maybe they'd even be right. I don't know about any of that, only that I feel safe with Rusalka—*cherished*—in a way I've never felt with another person. "I know," I finally manage. "But I want to stay. I feel more at home here than . . . anywhere else."

"Then your home this shall be." They kiss my temple. "We have so much time, little one. Slow down and cherish your days where no one is asking anything of you."

Except they are, aren't they? Not explicitly, not anymore, but I know the need this territory has. I understand the basics of warfare, if only vaguely. A baby isn't a nuke, but the concept's the same. If everyone has one, the respective territories are less likely to deploy them.

I've spent my whole life prepared for the fact that eventually I'd be a mother so some God-fearing man would be able to continue his genetic legacy, so good Christian folks would outnumber the heathens threatening the church's very way of life. Which is all really gross now that I'm thinking about it with a little distance. Having a baby for a territory of people who have welcomed me without hesitation, who have gone out of their way to ensure I feel just as safe with them as I do with Rusalka? That's different.

Yes, I haven't met every person in the territory. But even if the rest of them are jerks, Zhenya and Inna and Danik and Bogdan? The children whose free laughter I hear periodically throughout the day when I'm working in the gardens? They're all worth saving. They're worth *protecting*. I never thought of myself as a protector. The term doesn't sit easily on my shoulders, but it feels kind of right. I think?

"Belladonna?"

I've learned enough in the last week to know that this conversation is better left for another day. I don't want to argue with Rusalka when we're having such a wonderful time—especially when we really want the same thing.

I nuzzle her neck. "Sorry, I was gathering wool, or whatever that saying is." The truth, more or less.

Rusalka draws a spiral at the small of my back. "You've had a long day in a series of long days. Rest, Belladonna. You deserve it."

Their words ping against something deep inside me. I feel like my entire world has been changed since coming here, but there are still issues buried in the center of me that I don't know how to unpack. I don't know if I even want to. Apparently the concept of being deserving of rest is one of them.

I roll onto my back, bringing her with me. "You're in my bed. I don't want to rest. You promised me an entire night, and dawn is still hours away."

She settles between my thighs with a casual grace that takes my breath away. "It feels like you're running from something, little one."

Maybe. Probably. "It's not shame. I like what we do, and I

care about you." *More than care.* "I'm not running away from regret, either, if that's what you're worried about."

"Hmm."

It feels like she's seeing me too clearly, but then, she always sees me too clearly. It's something that I cherish and dread at the same time.

Finally, Rusalka kisses me. "You've trusted me this far, and so I'll trust that you'll tell me if this becomes something you use to harm yourself." Before I can come up with a response to that, they grin against my lips. "And I'll admit that I'm nowhere near done with you. If you're determined not to rest?" She laughs, low and wicked. "So be it."

Their flames lick over my body as they kiss me. They're all warmth and pressure and the occasional little flick of pain that makes it feel all the better. With another person, in another situation, I'd be terrified of being burned, but with Rusalka, I give myself over to their ministrations with gleeful abandon. It's all pleasure, even the small pains.

They push back, creating a little distance between our bodies. I immediately reach for them. "More."

"I'll give you more, little one." Their tone is amused in a way that makes me feel as though I'm in on the joke instead of the butt of it. "Trust me."

"I do," I say without hesitation. "With anything. With everything."

Their expression flickers so quickly, I almost miss the change. I'm too far gone to worry about what it means, especially when the fire licks over my body and gathers at Rusalka's hips. I watch with wide eyes as the flames wraps around her, pools in front, then forms . . . *"A strap-on."*

Another of those low laughs that make my toes curl. "This is so much more than that." She rolls her hips, pressing that fiery phallus into me, just a little. Warmth and a deep pleasure steal my thoughts and what little trepidation I might have had. Rusalka pauses. "My fire amplifies pleasure, and what you're feeling echoes through me, *in* me. It's . . ." They trail off, their eyes flickering again as they press a little farther into me, farther into themself.

"Good. Really good." I grip their hips, arching up to meet them. "More. Please."

"I'll give you as much as you can handle." She shifts me onto my left side and presses my right thigh up, opening me obscenely . . . and allowing her to settle even deeper inside me. Deep enough that her pussy presses to mine. Deep enough that her vibrating clitoris rubs against me, seeming to pulse through my entire core. Then she begins to move.

I've spent a number of guilt-ridden nights sneaking porn on my phone, enough to know the beats of penetrative sex and what to expect. My sole experience was similar enough, albeit without the screaming orgasms the women in those videos seem to have on command.

This is . . . different. Slower. More sensual. Rusalka is barely moving, just slightly rocking our hips in tandem as her wings create a heatless inferno at her back. Her flames hit that wicked spot inside me as her vibrations pulse faster. *"Oh."* It's like a flip is switched. All my bones go melty and strange, my muscles incapable of doing anything but clinging to her. "That feels so good."

"You should always feel good, little one." They kiss me before I can come up with a response, which is just as well. I don't know what I'd say to that. It's the antithesis of what I've grown up believing, and even as much as I want to embrace it wholeheartedly, I can't. Not yet. But maybe someday.

Rusalka doesn't pick up their pace, kissing me as they work me closer and closer to an orgasm unlike any I've experienced to date, building, building, building. Their breath comes just as fast as mine, their perfect breasts so close that I can't stop myself from cupping them. I pluck desperately at their nipples, which only serves to make their vibrations stronger. "Oh my . . . *Rusalka.*"

And then the pleasure isn't building but exploding inside me like a firework show, too bright and beautiful to witness, something I have to close my eyes against. That doesn't stop words from bursting out of me, though—the very words I swore I'd keep contained no matter what.

"I love you!"

20

RUSALKA

Hours and hours spent wrapped up in Belladonna, and when the morning finally comes, I can't ignore her words any longer. *I love you.* I stare down at the human, her now-short hair flung across her pillow, her limbs slack with sleep, her expression relaxed in a way it never seems to be during waking hours.

I know better than to take those words at face value. It's only been a week, and a tumultuous one at that. Love has happened faster on occasion, so it's not that I don't believe in the feeling. I have no doubt *she* believes it.

The circumstances give me pause, though. My Insomnior Court and I are, by all accounts, the first true kindness she's experienced without some kind of ulterior motive . . . Except we do have an ulterior motive, don't we? I made her wait a week to make her decision about having a baby, but if she still wants to do it, I can't say no. If I did, my people would be justified in asking me to step down as leader, and the next leader *would* accept Belladonna's sacrifice.

I trace my claws just above her body, a bare inch away from her skin so as not to wake her. No, I won't let someone else make that choice. If she insists on doing this thing, then I'll have to allow her to do it.

But love?

For a moment, I allow myself to picture it. A life where she stays, where we have a child or multiple children, whether she bears them or I do, or maybe neither of us. A life spent striving for peace, both internal and external. And, sometime far in the future, two old folks sitting in the shade and watching the people we love flourish.

Want wells up inside me, a deep and all-consuming thing. It doesn't make sense to crave that future with a woman I barely know, but I'm not the kind of person who spends overmuch time worrying about what *should* be, only what *is*.

I care deeply about Belladonna, and I want a future with her. I want her to stay. I want to *keep* her and for her to keep me, whatever that may look like for us.

It scares me how desperately I want that.

She stirs, her eyes slowly blinking open. "What time is it?"

"Too early with how late we fell asleep."

Her lips curve in a satisfied smile that makes my heart flip. "It's worth it."

She stretches slowly, arching her back in a way that makes my mouth go dry even though I know without a shadow of a doubt that she's not trying to seduce me. She shifts onto her side and studies me. "You look like you're thinking very hard about something."

"Nothing that needs to be talked about now." I don't want to do anything to bruise this lovely moment. Any talk of the future will do that. Instead, I brush her newly shorn hair back from her face. "I know you enjoy spending time in the gardens, but I was hoping to steal you away for the day."

The plan comes together as I say it. I've been intent on sharing her with as many of my people as possible, for both her and their benefit. But after last night, I'm feeling a bit selfish. I want to keep her attention all for myself.

"Steal me away?" She smiles wider. "What did you have in mind?"

I didn't have anything in mind when I said it, but suddenly there's an easy and perfect answer. "I want to take you shopping."

Instantly, she withdraws. Not physically, aside from the slightest flinch, but walls come down between us. Gods, I can almost see the poisonous whispers in the back of her mind, can imagine their shape and viciousness.

"Belladonna." I don't mean to put a snap into my voice, but it works—she meets my eyes, and she's here with me, not with *them* in that dark past. I hold her gaze. "We don't have to do anything you don't want to do. I will never force you into *anything*. But before you say no, I would like you to take a moment and think about what you really want—not what you think you should want."

She sighs and flops onto her back. "I'm that transparent?"

"In some ways." In others, I feel like no matter how hard I strive, I can't quite reach her. "If you don't want to go shopping, we can do something else."

She's silent long enough that I know she's actually thinking about it, which is all that I ask. Finally, she nods. "I do want this. I can't promise that I won't go dark during the process, but I'll do my best to be in the moment instead of worrying about what I *should* be doing." She takes my hand and laces her fingers through mine. "Though if you really want to keep me distracted, I can think of a few ways."

I almost tease her about being insatiable, but I don't

want that to come across as a criticism, so I just press her down onto the bed. We have plenty of daylight left. No reason not to enjoy ourselves ...

It's a full two hours later when we finally manage to shower off the evidence of our time in bed and dress. Belladonna has a secret smile that pulls at the edges of her lips whenever she looks at me, and I find myself returning it without thought. Giddiness takes hold as I lead her to the portal tucked away in the basement, behind armored guards. The portal that conveys us to Azazel's city-state.

Ramanu is waiting for us the moment we step through, their smile self-satisfied, as if they've won a bet. "Good morning. You look like you slept ... well."

I roll my eyes. "Yes, yes, you're very observant. We're here for a day trip."

"Of course." They motion gracefully for the door. "I'll escort you out of the castle. When you're ready to return to the portal, ask one of the guards at the door to fetch me."

Belladonna watches them with wide eyes, but there's no fear coloring her desires. There's more a caution that makes me think Ramanu found some time to poke holes in the "truths" drilled into her from birth. They guide us through the corridors to a large arched double door. "Azazel may be free by the time you're done."

"Tell him not to worry himself on my account." Even as I say it, I know there's no escaping this. It was all but fated from the moment I decided to bring Belladonna here. He's going to want to check on her personally, and I can't fault him for his concern even if I resent it. She's not his, not any longer. I don't give a fuck what the contract says.

"You know better." Ramanu laughs a little. "Enjoy the city. I'll see you in a bit."

Belladonna doesn't speak until we're well away from the castle. The city always seems to be bustling, demons going about their business. She watches everything with interest for several blocks before glancing at me. "They're the only one I've seen with . . ." She motions to her eyes.

"Ramanu is half bargainer demon and half gargoyle."

"Oh." She says it slowly. "What happens if human is added to the mix?"

I should have known we wouldn't be able to avoid this question indefinitely. I wrap up my frustration and tuck it away. "Humans have a tendency to birth babies more humanoid than not, regardless of their partner. It's how all the peoples of this realm came to be."

"*What?*"

This is easier to talk about. Preferable, even. I slide my arm around her shoulders and tuck her against my body as we walk. "I'm sure you've noticed that most of us here are humanoid, give or take some tentacles and a tail or two. It's because some ancestor of yours wandered on the wild side and fucked a dragon, or a kraken, or a gargoyle, or . . . well, fire and shadows."

Her eyes are massive in her face as she says, "Your ancestors are fire and shadows."

"And lust." I laugh. "Legend has it that we were more incorporeal in those days, living mostly in dreams. I'm not sure how my ancestors surpassed that barrier to impregnate a human—or be impregnated by one—but it happened, and often enough that here we are, all these generations later."

Belladonna seems a little shell-shocked as I guide her

into the first store, a suit shop that I favor when I have cause to be in the city. She stops just inside the door. "Wait, I suppose I could understand incubi and succubi, but you also said *dragons* and *kraken*. Weren't they . . ." She holds her arms wide.

"Yes."

If anything, her eyes get wider. "That's . . . How did that work?"

"That, little one, is a question for another day."

21

BELLADONNA

It takes Rusalka some time to coax me into trying on the clothes she's picked for me, and even more time before I feel confident enough to step out of the changing room with an outfit on to show her. It's strange that I've been naked in front of her but somehow this feels more intimate. She's *dressing* me.

I run my hands over the luxurious red fabric and meet their gaze. "This is too much."

"It pleases me to spoil you." They lounge in a chair a few feet away, one long leg draped over the arm. "Really, you're doing *me* a favor by allowing me to purchase clothing for you."

"That logic is really ridiculous, but I recognize that it's not an argument I'm going to win." It strikes me as I slip back into the changing room that I've adjusted to their cloven hooves and tail—I hardly notice them as strange features anymore.

One by one, I try on the pieces she sends me. One by one, I step out to show them each piece. Every time, they tell me how perfect the clothing is on me, how beautiful I look . . . how they can't wait to strip me out of it and have their wicked way with me. The praise makes me uncomfortable, but I can't deny the heat that begins beneath my skin, promising more.

I hurriedly pull my normal clothing back on and pass the last dress to the salesperson who's been hovering discreetly. "Thank you."

They bob their head, a small smile on their lips. They look similar to Azazel, but only superficially so—red skin and horns, though their horns curl back more like those of a ram than a bull. Their body is slighter, like Ramanu's, and their skin is several shades closer to purple than true red.

I cross to Rusalka. "Take me home, Rusalka." My voice catches in the middle of the sentence. My skin feels as though it's on fire. "Please. So we can . . . you know."

She pulls me close and brushes a light kiss to my lips. "One day, you'll be able to tell me explicitly what you want." She slips an arm around my waist. "But for now, trust that I will take care of you, little one. I'll see to every single need."

"Yes. Please." Need is a living thing inside me. It's not Rusalka's magic; thatfeels more like I imagine being drunk would; everything goes hazy and warm and fluid. Right now, the world around me stands out in sharp focus. I can almost measure the distance back to the portal in the beats of my racing heart. "Or maybe we don't wait?"

Rusalka shakes their head. "As much as I would love to drag you into that dressing room and see whether your embarrassment or my tongue would win, we're in enemy territory."

"*Enemy.*" I have to stop and make a conscious decision to lower my voice. "But Azazel is the reason I'm here. He's trying—"

"I know." They smooth a hand down my back. "'Enemy'

may be too strong a word. But a certain amount of caution is warranted. There's always the chance, however small, that this is all an elaborate trap. If last night is any indication, when I'm with you, I lose all sense of time and place. That's a blessing in our home—and a risk outside it."

I was there. I don't know why it's so shocking to hear that Rusalka enjoyed her time with me so much that she lost herself just like I lost myself. What she's saying makes sense, but that doesn't stop the heat from rising beneath my skin. As much as I want her . . . she wants me too? I press my thighs together. "Are you sure?"

Rusalka stops and looks down at me. Their amber eyes widen, and they smile. "You little troublemaker. You like the idea of distracting me to potentially deadly consequences."

"Not *deadly*." I shake my head rapidly. "I don't want anything to happen to you—or to the territory. But yes, I guess I do like the idea of being wanted that much."

One moment, I'm standing there, looking up at them. The next, my back hits the wall in the dressing room and the curtain swishes shut. It happened so fast, I didn't even feel us move. I blink up at her. "I didn't know you could move like that."

"I can when motivated." Rusalka kisses me, pressing me harder against the wall. "We have to be quick."

The sparks beneath my skin turn into an inferno. Before, Rusalka was so careful with me, so patient. There's none of that now. We're a flurry of questing hands shoving fabric aside and little gasps swallowed between needy mouths. They find my molten core first, press a finger inside, and grind the heel of their hand against my clitoris. Pleasure makes me fumble even more, but I manage to get their pants down their hips enough to find what I'm looking for.

I moan when I find them wet. They clamp around my

finger and press their forehead hard to mine. "Faster, little one. Harder."

I don't know what I'm doing. I fingered her a little during the marathon lovemaking, but that was more teasing than trying to make her orgasm. But she's showing me the way, isn't she? I try to match her rhythm, her grinding thrusts that I swear I can feel in the back of my throat and all the way to my toes.

My orgasm slams into me, too fast, too hard, too *brutal*. Rusalka swallows down my cry, and then she's grinding hard against my touch, her pussy clenching around my fingers, her clitoris vibrating against my skin, her wetness soaking my hand. She . . . orgasmed . . . in a dressing room . . . because of *me*.

I push them down onto the small bench and go to my knees between their thighs. Rusalka opens their mouth like they might protest, but I shove their pants down around their ankles and cover their center with my mouth. So wet. Because of *me*. I didn't know I could feel possessive like this. Surely someone would call it a sin, but I don't care about anything but Rusalka's hands in my hair and their head falling back in submission to what I'm doing to them.

It's not true submission, not with her guiding me with a tension that has the flavor of silent command. I eagerly follow, thrusting my tongue into her before rolling the flat of it against her vibrating clit just the way she showed me she likes. It's only a few moments before her thighs go tight on either side of my head and she comes all over my face. I keep going. I can't help it. I don't think I'll ever get enough of her taste, of the way her whole body shivers when she comes. I need . . .

"Enough." She says it on a breathless laugh. "You're going to get us in trouble."

"Worth it," I murmur. But I let her tug me up her body and kiss me deeply. My orgasm barely took the edge off my need, and so I have to use what little self-control I have left to hold still as Rusalka puts our clothes to rights and takes my hand. We share a secret smile . . .

Which dies the moment we step out of the dressing room and find Azazel himself waiting for us.

He is wearing an outfit similar to the last one I saw him in: a wrap around his hips, boots, and little else. His horns nearly drag along the ceiling, and his expression is forbidding enough that I'm tempted to shrink behind Rusalka.

Except hiding will all but admit I think we're doing something wrong, and I fucking *refuse*. We are two consenting adults. Yes, maybe having sex in a semipublic place was a little ill-advised, but it wasn't *wrong*. It wasn't shameful.

I don't make a conscious decision to step in front of Rusalka. My body does it on its own. As I look up to meet Azazel's dark eyes, I think I might pass out on the spot if he looks angry.

He doesn't. There's a caution there that he wore even in his human skin, and something I can't quite define, but no anger.

I say, "It's not their fault."

"No one is speaking about fault," he rumbles. "I came to see for myself what Ramanu tells me is true. Apparently they're correct." His gaze shifts to Rusalka and softens a little. "I'm glad to see I made the right call."

I don't really know what that means, but it's obvious we're not in trouble. I don't know what to do with that. The adrenaline rushes from my body in a whoosh that leaves me dizzy. The room spins, and both Azazel and Rusalka rush to grab me as I start to tilt.

Rusalka hisses at Azazel. Actually *hisses*. "I've got her."

He instantly raises both hands and takes a step back. "I see that. I meant no disrespect."

There are layers upon layers here, and I don't know what to do with that. So I ignore the whole thing. I look up at Rusalka. "Can we go home? Please."

"Yes," they say slowly, but their attention is on Azazel. "As I told Ramanu, we merely came to avail ourselves of your shops. They have styles I thought would appeal to Belladonna. Nothing more insidious than that."

He sighs, his shoulders relaxing a little. "No need to tiptoe around me. I'm not here to play games. I wanted to check in." He glances at me. "And to invite you both to dinner."

I expect Rusalka to tell him no, but they smile. "Dinner sounds lovely."

I wish I could say the same.

22

RUSALKA

My irritation at Azazel's ambush lasts until we arrive at a medium-sized round table. I've attended state dinners here on occasion, and at those, we always dine at a massive beast of a table where you have no hope of talking to the people on the other side. Clever when it comes to having borderline-warring leaders attend. This is different—intimate. This is where the demon king eats when he's not trying to impress anyone.

Which begs the question of why he's brought *us* here.

I hold a chair out for Belladonna and give her shoulder a squeeze before I perch on the chair next to her, positioning myself between her and Azazel. I don't think for a moment that he's a threat to her, but she's practically quivering with nerves, and I don't want her to be more uncomfortable than she has to be.

I point to the fourth plate across from me. "Is someone else joining us?"

"Perhaps." A new tension tightens his shoulders, telling a story if one cares to look.

Normally, I wouldn't say anything, out of courtesy, but fuck that. I would rather be back in my territory, coaxing Belladonna into screaming my name a dozen times before dawn. I tap my claws on the table. "You took the fifth woman."

He flinches. It's a tiny movement, practically microscopic, but I see it all the same.

I lean forward. "You did, didn't you? But why? That must be against your lauded bargainer demon morals."

"It wasn't against my morals to add a secondary bargain to the others." He nods at Belladonna.

"Cute dodge, but a dodge nonetheless. Your bargains bring the humans here, and then you allow them to find the work they're happiest with."

He narrows his eyes. "And here I thought they were all sexual workers by contract."

"Don't play with me. That might be what the others think, but I know better. You're precious about your humans, and I wager most of them aren't suited to sex work or wouldn't choose it if there were a choice—and there *is* a choice." I grin. "It's interesting that you're still dodging my question, though."

"Leave it alone, Rusalka." He turns that fearsome glare on Belladonna but seems to try to temper it. "You seem well. Are you enjoying your time with Rusalka?"

He knows damn well exactly how much she is—and what challenges we've faced. Ramanu reports everything they learn on their check-ins to Azazel. That was part of the contract I agreed to. I don't point it out, though. This is a small kindness, to give Belladonna the courtesy of asking instead of lording his knowledge over both of us.

Azazel's a pain in the ass, but I can't fault him in his treatment of those under his power.

"I, uh . . ." She glances at me, her eyes a little too wide.

I reach over beneath the table and clasp her hand. "It's okay. You can talk freely. Azazel isn't going to sweep in and take you away from us."

"Unless you want me to," he rumbles.

"No!" Belladonna clears her throat. "No, that won't be necessary. I'm enjoying my time with Rusalka and her court and the people I've met in town." Her grip is so tight on my hand that it grinds my bones together. I don't like the way her nerves saturate the very air around us. It's a change, and not a welcome one. She wasn't afraid of Azazel when I met her. What's changed?

Azazel pauses as a servant comes in and pours deep glasses of wine. *Four* deep glasses of wine. I give the empty seat a significant look, but Belladonna speaks before I can question him further. She eyes the wine and gives him a tentative smile. "I've been spending time in the gardens. I find it very relaxing, and I'm learning a lot from Bogdan."

"Bogdan." He chuckles. "Even I know his fearsome reputation. The board of gardeners for Odonhert once bargained with him for a specific variety of flower he had grafted or . . ." He waves a hand in a charming helpless motion. "I'll admit that I'm out of my depth when it comes to the topic. But the flower increased pollination capacity or something to that effect. He drove a hard enough bargain that my people still talk about it."

The Insomnior Court still talks about it, too, though not with quite that flavor of admiration. Bogdan hadn't wanted to make a deal at all. I spent weeks persuading him to even see the bargainer demons and then ran myself so ragged during their time in my village that I was incapacitated for a solid week after they left. Not sick, at least not with any illness, but riddled with an exhaustion so intense, I could barely get out of bed.

But we got a good deal out of the mess, one that's benefited us to this day, so I counted the cost worth it.

Belladonna's grip relaxes slightly in mine. "You sound almost admiring."

"I am. Bargains are sacred among my people." He lifts his wine, the glass looking absurdly small in his massive hand, and takes a sip. "I trust both parties came away pleased with the bargain."

"They were," I say. "We gained access to a new technology that none of the other territories possess, and the bargainers have had a particularly bountiful harvest in the years since they put the flower into circulation."

The sound of a door opening causes all three of us to turn as a short blond woman with pale skin and a curvy body walks into the room. She pointedly doesn't look at Azazel while she moves to the table and delicately sinks into the chair across from me. She's pretty, bordering on beautiful, but there's a deep unhappiness in her that feels like a prickly weight against my skin. It's evident in the way she downs half the wine in a single drink, in the tension in her shoulders, in the shadows beneath her eyes.

Azazel clears his throat. "This is Eve. Eve, this is Rusalka and Belladonna."

"I remember you." Eve looks at Belladonna, some of the tightness fading from her expression. "You were part of the auction."

"Yes." Belladonna leans forward. "It's been an interesting experience."

"Interesting. That's one way to put it." Eve finishes her glass fast enough that I can't help looking at Azazel. Surely she's too small to be downing demon wine so quickly without consequences. The look on his face stops me short. I've never seen such yearning. And it's combined with resignation and a slow-building fury that makes me want to get Belladonna out of here as quickly as possible. We may have nothing to fear from Azazel, but that doesn't mean seeing him yell at his prickly human won't upset Belladonna.

But in the span of that realization, Belladonna has made one of her own. She sits back and extracts her hand from mine so she can cross her arms over her chest. "You're not happy here."

"Ding, ding, ding." Eve raises her glass, but Azazel shakes his head and moves the bottle out of reach. She shrugs and reaches over to grab his glass. He tries to catch her wrist, but she's too quick, easily slipping from his grasp.

Belladonna frowns harder. "If you're being mistreated—"

"Mind your tongue," Azazel growls.

That sparks my anger. "I don't care if you made the initial deal that got her here. If you use that tone again, I'll rip out *your* tongue."

Eve laughs bitterly. "Down, *Daddy*." She turns to address Belladonna, some of the venom in her tone eases. "Thank you for your concern, but I'm fine. I'm *safe*." She practically spits the word. "What reason do I have to be angry?"

Azazel sighs. "Eve . . ."

"I think I've had enough. Good night." She rises unsteadily to her feet, sweeping up Belladonna's wine as she does, and wobbles out of the room.

Even with the magic of the castle, I don't like her chances of making it back to her room without issue. I glance at Azazel, but he's already rising. "I apologize. This isn't how I'd hoped things would go. I have to see to Eve."

"Wait."

He pauses and looks at Belladonna, who seems horrified that she barked a command at him. "Yes?"

She swallows visibly. "I know you said time moves differently, but . . . My sister?"

The frustration in his expression disappears, but the feeling compounds out of sight, where only I can see it. "She was gifted with an anonymous medical scholarship to cover her treatment the moment you signed the deal." His lips twist, apparently despite his best efforts. "Your parents believe it's a reward for her faith that your god would provide."

"Not my god. Not anymore." Belladonna shakes a little but nods. "Thank you for telling me."

"Of course." He turns toward the door once more. "Stay as long as you like. One of my people will escort you to the portal when you're ready to go." He stalks out of the room, eating up the distance between him and Eve, whom I can hear using the wall to walk her way down the hall.

Belladonna throws her napkin on the table. "Can we go now?"

"Absolutely." I rise and take her hand. "No reason to linger."

We barely make it out the door before Ramanu appears, looking a little frazzled. Or as frazzled as they ever get. "Please follow me."

I wait until we're down within throwing distance of the portal to dig in my heels. "Ramanu."

"I know."

"No, I don't think you do. What the *fuck* was that about?" In all my years of knowing Azazel, I would have bet a large amount of money that he'd never take a bargain with someone who truly doesn't want it. The way he's handled Belladonna only reinforces that truth.

What I just witnessed with Eve contradicts all of that.

Ramanu scrubs their hands over their horns. "It's complicated."

"Uncomplicate it." I glance at Belladonna. "I'm sorry, little one. I know you don't want to make waves, but this is worrisome."

"It's okay." She squeezes my hand and nods at Ramanu. "Eve seems deeply unhappy."

"She is." Ramanu sighs and props their hands on their hips. "I'm only sharing this because I know you won't leave it alone."

"Accurate."

"I know." They shake their head. "Eve and Azazel have . . . history. They knew each other before the deal. He wasn't entirely honest in his negotiations for her contract. She isn't taking it well. She's upset, but she's safe, and the expected rules of the contract hold." They nod at the packages sitting next to the portal. "Your things are there. I'll be around in the next couple of weeks to check in again."

Belladonna frowns. "Weeks? Why so long?"

"I have a task that needs tending to." Their grin goes wolfish. "A little witch is in need of my help."

" . . . Oh."

"If you need anything, of course, you can always contact Azazel."

She shakes her head rapidly. "That won't be necessary."

"We'll see." They step out of the way and motion for us to move past.

I waste no time gathering up our things and urging Belladonna through the portal ahead of me. Azazel has his hands full, even if it's with a situation of his own making. I don't envy him the battle ahead, especially when every time he looked at Eve, his longing filled up the room until I could barely breathe past it. There's desire and there's *desire*, and the latter going unfulfilled for too long will only sour and end in misery for everyone. I truly hope he figures it out before that point.

As for me? I have a precious little human to take to bed.

23

BELLADONNA

The days slip by, one after the other, there and gone in a pleasant bliss that feels as though a spell is wrapped around me. It's not. I've learned the sensation of Rusalka's magic and how it differs from the others in their Insomnior Court. I've chosen not to ask to attend any of the parties since the first, but I sometimes hear the festivities late in the night when I'm sprawled next to Rusalka, letting their breathing soothe something in me that I didn't know was broken.

I spend my days in the garden. Bogdan is only a little grumpy; I don't know what Azazel was going on about. He's practically an angel as far as I'm concerned, with endless patience, even on days when children start to filter into the garden, all barely constrained curiosity about me and enthusiasm for digging in the dirt.

When he gets gruff—and he *never* gets gruff with the kids—he never raises his voice or makes remarks about my value as a human being or tells me that I'm disappointing him. It's as healing as my nights with Rusalka to have someone correct me without hurting me in the process.

And time with the children . . . They're their own kind of healing. They are all so different, from Brin, with her love of pretty dresses ansd flowers in her hair, to Mac, who thinks every problem can be solved with his fire powers, to quiet Sari, who is content to kneel at my side and mimic my movements, their orange eyes wide and excited to be allowed to help with "adult things" like weeding.

There's no fear in them. No shame. They are growing up free and loved by every adult around them, cherished and protected. I didn't know it could be like this. When my mind wanders while my fingers are in the dirt, I catch myself wondering what *my* child might be like raised in a community this willing to hold them with love and care.

The thought of having children to feed into the church, to raise its numbers, to prepare for a holy war that might never come . . . it filled me with a dread I don't know how to quantify.

But having a child *here*? That's a completely different feeling. That's a future that fills my chest with such hope, it could make me weep. There is cruelty, even in this realm, but at least any child of mine would be protected until they were old enough to face that cruelty without being broken by it.

Until they were old enough to step into a leadership position to further protect the children that will come after them.

Even with those thoughts—those possibilities—circling closer every day, I put off having the conversation with Rusalka about a baby, and then I put it off again. It's not that I'm not becoming more and more enamored with the idea of having a child here, or that I don't want to help the people who have welcomed me into their community without hesitation. I want both. It's just . . . this life is *nice*.

I'm not quite ready for it to end, to change.

That thought continues to take up residence in my mind in the couple of weeks after our awkward dinner with Azazel. I try to root it out as I weed the section of the gardens Bogdan has assigned me for the day, but it's not as eager to submit as the little shoots of purple grass in moist soil are. The children are off on a chaperoned hike today—a lovely way to burn off some of their endless energy—and their absence is giving me too much time to think.

More thoughts circle and circle, taking bites out of me with each pass. I try to ignore them, but it's not like ignoring the horrible things my parents and Pastor John used to say to me under the guise of looking out for my immortal soul. Those voices still plague me, but they're getting fainter every day. But these words? They're *mine*. An admission of selfishness that I can't quite escape.

There's no reason to wait. A baby will secure this territory and its people. Yes, it means my purpose will have been served. But that's a good thing, isn't it?

Though maybe Rusalka won't be as interested in me if she's not worried about the future of her people. Maybe the townsfolk won't be as kind once I've given them what they want. Maybe they'll start acting more familiar, wielding cutting words and judgment. Maybe they'll start keeping their children from the gardens, not wanting them around me.

Or maybe that's my fear talking.

Maybe . . .

I take a breath and press my hands to the soil. I can't actually feel the steady beat of the earth the way Bogdan says he can, but he also says my impatience is the reason, not the fact that I'm human and flawed. So I wait, and wait, and wait some more. I don't know if I feel the earth's heart beating, but I manage to breathe deeply enough that my spiraling thoughts slow to a crawl.

"Maybe," I whisper, then pause to make sure I'm actually alone. It seems particularly perilous to speak my hope out loud, but I want my words to feel real. "Maybe having a baby won't change anything for the bad. Maybe all the good things I've experienced since coming here are actually true and Rusalka could grow to care for me as much as I care for . . ." I take a deep breath. "As much as I *love* her."

The situation still seems impossible, but I tuck that small kernel of hope deep inside me. The sensation feels fragile and strange, but not in a bad way.

That kernel and the soothing experience of weeding the space to prepare for new growth keep the worries at bay through the rest of the day. Mostly.

I don't see anyone as I walk into the manor house and head upstairs to bathe before dinner. I technically still have my room, but with each night that's passed without my returning to it, Rusalka's bedroom starts to feel more like *ours*. She's even made space for my newly purchased clothes in her closet.

Washing away the dirt from my day always feels a little bittersweet. The dirt is evidence of how hard I worked, of what progress I made, but it feels *so good* to have freshly cleaned skin—especially with the decadent lotions Rusalka keeps in the bathroom.

I'm just pulling on one of my favorite dresses—another red and flowing piece that makes me feel part princess and part succubus—when Rusalka walks into the room. The moment they see me, they cross to me and pull me into their arms for a devastating kiss.

It's over much too quickly, but she only leans back a little instead of releasing me. "You look good enough to eat."

"You, too," I manage breathlessly. They're wearing loose trousers and a fitted sleeveless top that shows off their muscular shoulders in a way that, strangely, makes me want to bite them. Sexually. "How was your day?"

"Long." Rusalka leans back a little and props her chin on the top of my head. "A pack of hellcats wandered too close to a neighboring village. We do our best not to kill them unnecessarily, but they're incredibly dangerous, especially when they have kits, which this pack does. The moment the village's children realize they're close, they'll do something foolish, and then we'll have too much death on our hands."

"Oh no. That's terrible."

"It's okay. I think we have a plan for relocation that will be successful. It's just going to require speed and careful handling." They squeeze me. "How are the gardens?"

"The bright berries are sprouting. Bogdan says it will be months before their fruit even shows up, let alone is ripe enough to pick and eat, but it's still really exciting."

Rusalka smiles. "That is. Jitka makes the best bright berry pie I've ever had the privilege of eating. We haven't had any since you've arrived because she prefers to make it with fresh bright berry instead of frozen or dried. It's a life-changing experience."

"Speaking of life-changing experiences." I don't mean to say it. Truly, I don't. I may have spent all day thinking about the future and existing in the space between fear and hope, but that doesn't mean I want to ruin this. It's too late to go back now, though. I clear my throat. "We haven't talked about the baby in weeks."

"There is no baby to speak of," they say gently. "It's a concept, and barely one at that."

"Rusalka."

She sighs and releases me. "I'm enjoying my time with you. I think you're enjoying your time with me as well."

I swallow hard. "I am."

"Then why rush this? We *have* time."

How is it possible that I love her all the more because she's obviously trying to protect me . . . at the expense of her people? I can't ask her to do that. I *won't*. "I want a baby." I finally say the words I've been chewing on for days and days, the truth that was so deep, I was afraid to face it.

"Do you?" They turn away from me. "Or do you just want a purpose?"

The words sting. More than sting. They slice deeply into the heart of me. It hurts so much that I actually gasp. "That's not fair."

"Life's not fair, little one."

I should tell them that I want this baby for the sake of having a child so loved that they have nothing to fear. That I want a baby with Rusalka, who will be a full and caring partner no matter what the future between us may bring, who will inspire our child with her fearlessness and confidence.

Except I don't say that. If I put that fragile fantasy of a future into words and she rejects me, I don't think I'll survive it. "I'm trying to help," I finally whisper.

"Then help yourself!" Rusalka has never raised their voice in my presence. They've never come undone with anger the way they are now. "I thought you were happy, Belladonna. I thought we were making progress. I . . ." They run their hands through their short hair. "I need to think. I'm going for a walk."

My mouth works, but with my throat closing, I don't get words out before Rusalka is gone. She left me. I shake my head, hard. No, she didn't leave me. That's nonsense. That's my fear talking. She just . . . stormed out in the middle of a conversation that hadn't even been long enough to be termed an argument. She needed to leave the building entirely because her frustration at me was too over-whelming.

I hate how familiar this feeling of abandonment is. I hate how it instantly shoves me back into a skin I hadn't even been aware I was shedding. The old urge to hide, to make myself small, is almost overwhelming. I actually start to take off my dress and look for sleeping clothes, mentally trace my path down to the room I haven't slept in for weeks.

Only to stop short. "What am I doing?" Is Rusalka angry at me . . . or is she angry *for* me? I don't know. If there's a difference, I don't know how to divine it. Not without asking them. I stare at the door. I have never, not once, pursued a conversation when someone angry at me walked away in a fury. The idea of facing that fear is terrifying on a level I can barely comprehend. But this isn't my mother, my father, the church community. This isn't Ruth, who would never yell, but would tell me that she needs time away from me in order to pray away her frustration.

This is Rusalka.

And Rusalka would never hurt me. Not on purpose.

"Fuck this." I shove open the door and step into the hall.

24

RUSALKA

I'm filled with regret from the moment I leave the room, but that's still not enough to stop my forward momentum. I'm a fool. I thought we were making progress, that Belladonna might actually want a *future* with me. I know it's too fucking soon, that it's not fair to expect her to have shed a lifetime's worth of trauma in the span of a few weeks.

But I wanted her to want more for herself than to be an empty womb to be filled in the service of others. I *still* want that.

The stairs pass in a blur. There's a roaring in my head that eclipses everything. I'm feeling too much, and it's my own damned fault. Belladonna is going to think I'm furious at her, when really I'm angry at myself. If I were more ruthless, I wouldn't worry about what a pregnancy now, for the sole purpose of helping my territory, would do to this woman I only met a few weeks ago but care about far more than I could have dreamed. If I were a better leader, not even that worry would be enough to make me dissuade her.

But I don't want to be a leader who breaks *her*, even if it serves the greater good.

Except I didn't say that, did I?

I didn't tell Belladonna that I care about her and I'm worried about her. I just started yelling at her and then stormed off.

Even now, I'm not thinking clearly. She's going to think . . . Fuck, I just hurt her terribly, didn't I? It's going to reinforce all the awful stuff she's been so diligent about fighting in her head. Instead of being understanding, I just knocked her feet right out from under her.

I stop short and turn around, intent on returning to actually talk this out instead of letting emotions get the best of me. No matter what I find when I get back to our room—because the room has become *ours* and I don't want that to change—we'll work through it.

But, when I turn around, the hallway isn't empty. Belladonna is hurrying toward me, her expression intent. Shock stops me in my tracks. "You came after me."

"You ran away." She staggers to a stop a few feet from me, her breath coming hard. "I . . . Hold on." She plants her hands on her thighs. "I just need . . . a second."

"Take all the time you need," I say faintly. *She came after me.* With any of my Insomnior Court, this wouldn't be notable. We're all hotheads in our own way when the circumstances arise, but we know one another well enough to know when to let someone walk off some frustration and when distance is only going to make things worse.

But Belladonna isn't Zhenya or Inna or Danik. She doesn't have the benefit of years of experience with my temper, slow to anger though I may be. More importantly, in her history, she's been badgered and belittled and crushed into a smaller version of herself—someone who wouldn't have the courage to pursue a tough conversation that may not go her way, because nothing ever went her way while she was under the control of toxic people.

"You came after me," I can't help repeating.

"You." Belladonna finally straightens, though she's still breathing a little hard. "You didn't look like you were moving that fast, but you really were. I had to run to catch up with you."

"Sorry." I look away, but my gaze is drawn back to her almost instantly. I drag in a breath. "I really am sorry. I didn't—"

"No." She slices a hand through the air. "You will let *me* speak, and you won't run away in the middle of it."

Shock silences me for several beats. This is a side of Belladonna that I've never seen before, and I like it. A lot. "Okay."

"Oh, well, uh, good." She shoves her hair out of her face. "I'm not good at this, but I'm going to try."

I press my lips together as she attempts to compose herself. The urge to step closer, to touch her, to do whatever it takes to make things right, nearly overwhelms me. But Belladonna asked for space to speak, and giving it to her is the least I can do.

"I care about you," she says quietly. "More than care, if I'm being honest. We haven't talked about how my feelings sort of slipped out when we were having sex, which I appreciated in the moment, but now I'm wondering if we should have. It's not just sex to me. I don't know *how* it could be just sex. I *love* you, Rusalka. Not just because you make me feel good physically. Not just because you've been so intentional about creating a space for me to find my feet since I came here. Not just because you actually listen and gently counter some of the horrible truths I grew up taking to heart." She drags in a breath. "But also because you're a good person."

"Belladonna—"

"Let me finish. You *are* a good person. You take care of everyone around you, from Zhenya, Danik, and Inna to all your staff to the town to the territory. This territory doesn't need a human baby to turn it around—your leadership means your people are flourishing."

Heat rises beneath my skin. I have the strangest urge to look away, to curl my shoulders. "I don't do it for praise. It is the right thing to do."

"I know. That just makes me love you more." She lifts her hands as if she might reach for me but abandons the movement halfway through. "I want to help people, too. Not at the expense of myself, though. Not anymore."

As much as it heartens me to hear that, it doesn't change the fact that she offered to have a baby just a few minutes ago. "So you're going to drop the baby conversation."

She frowns. "That's not what I said."

"Then what *are* you saying?"

"I'm saying that . . ." She squares her shoulders. "There's nothing wrong with helping people. Maybe I haven't always wanted to do it for the right reasons, but that's still the truth. Aren't leaders supposed to prioritize the good of the many?"

Yes. Absolutely. Without a doubt. "I won't do that. Not when you're the one being hurt to benefit the many." I could leave it there, but she's been so damned brave. I can match that bravery. For her. "If I were a better leader, I would allow you to sacrifice yourself for the betterment of my territory. I would allow your child to be born solely to benefit us all, rather than because they were wanted. I won't, Belladonna. I love you, and I'll be damned if I allow any more pain into your life—or the life of an innocent baby. You should only experience peace and contentment and appreciation going forward. Never shame, never hurt."

Her eyes well a little, but not a single tear escapes. It kills me to wonder if that's a learned skill. I imagine her tears weren't met with empathy when it came to her family. Belladonna sniffs. "Could you say it again, please?"

"I love you."

She steps forward, wraps her arms around me. "I love you, too."

I don't know what to feel. I'm still angry, but I'm not angry *at* her. I'm elated that she's telling me she loves me outside the bedroom. I'm hopeful for the future. I'm terrified I'm going to fuck this up, in a way I've never been terrified of anything. "I want to kill your parents."

"What?" Belladonna blinks, then blinks again. "That would be . . . I think that may put you at odds with Azazel, considering my bargain."

"I know." I sigh. "I won't do it—even if they deserve it—because it would hurt you. Also because Danik refused to obey my order to find them. But the desire is there nonetheless."

"Thank you?" She shakes her head and hugs me tighter. "I don't want anyone hurt on my account."

"I know." That inherent goodness is part of what makes her *her*. "I want children, too. I know I've said that before, and it's true."

Belladonna smiles a little. "I do, too. Not just for other people, but for myself." She strokes her hands over my back. "I don't expect you to believe that—not yet—but it's the truth. The idea of raising a child here, of their having such an abundance of love in their life because of this community, because they have you as their parent . . . Rusalka, that sounds *fucking beautiful*?"

I hug her close and let her steady warmth soothe me. "There's no rush, little one. We have time. Why not enjoy each other for a little while longer? Why not wait until we both feel like it's the right time for *us*, rather than for other people?"

She pulls back a little. I don't like the new distance, but I get it—she obviously wants to read my expression. "You'd want children with me even if it wouldn't benefit the territory?"

"Yes." It's the truth. "I'm not sad that our children will create a more prosperous territory, but that's not *why* I want them."

"Then . . . I suppose it wouldn't hurt us to wait." She looks away and then back at me. "But I don't like how that fight went. We're going to fight—I don't think there's a way to avoid it—but . . ." She gulps down a breath. "Please don't walk away in the middle again, at least not without plans to resume the conversation if you need time to calm down. I can't handle that, Rusalka. It hurt."

"I'm sorry," I whisper. "It won't happen again." I had only thought to spare her my messy emotions, which was a bit selfish in hindsight. Isn't that always the way? We're all just doing our best, and sometimes we bruise the ones we most care about in the process. "I'll do better."

"We both will." She takes my hand and turns us back toward the stairs. "But, even if we're not going to have a baby soon, maybe we could . . . practice?"

I flush hot and then hotter. "Practice."

"I know we're choosing not to utilize a key component of the whole baby-making process, but I think that may make it more fun?" A blush takes up residence in her cheeks, and that only makes me need her more.s

I pick up my pace. "Yes. Practice sounds *perfect*."

EPILOGUE

BELLADONNA

"A re you sure?"

I smile at Rusalka, because it's the same question they've asked me a dozen times leading up to tonight. It doesn't matter that we've been together two full years now, or that we both knew this day would come. They still want me to be sure and safe in this decision. "I'm sure."

They eye the door we're about to walk through almost nervously. "If at any point you change your mind—"

"Rusalka." I wait for her to turn to face me fully and take her hands. "I want this for our people, yes, but I want this for *us*. You and me." I won't pretend that it's been the easiest path to get here. The insidious nature of my internal whispers still strike at the most unexpected times. It hurts. I don't think it will ever stop hurting entirely. But I have ways to deal with that pain now. I talk to Rusalka. I garden. I spend time with our people. There's even a therapist of sorts—a soul-healer, Rusalka calls nem—that I've been seeing. Jacquiel is good at asking questions and giving me ways to fight through to the other side. I like nem a lot—even when I hate nem.

All of this has brought us here, to this moment, to this party.

"Are *you* ready?" I squeeze her hands. "I know we've talked about this, but if you've changed your mind, I can keep the birth control pendant on and it can be a normal party like we've done in the past."

She takes a deep breath and pulls me into her arms to hug me close. "No, that's not it at all. I want this, too. You know how much. If you're sure, then I'm sure."

"I'm sure." It's the truth. Every day of the last two years has been filled with the kind of safety I barely dared dream about back in the human realm. There have been learning curves and Rusalka and I argue on a semi regular basis about various things, but those arguments have solutions and can be talked through. No one is leveraging threats of burning in an everlasting hell if I don't act according to rules I don't believe in.

"Then let's go." They push open the door and hold it for me to step into the room. It's the same one all the parties are held in, big and luxurious and filled with a variety of furniture to lounge on...or play on.

Zhenya sees us first and bounds over, only a sheer robe covering zir body. "You're here." Ze kisses me lightly on the lips and then does the same to Rusalka. "Let's have some fun!"

I share one last look with Rusalka before I'm swept away in Zhenya's enthusiasm. I'll find her at the end of the night, if not before. The concept of ethical non-monogamy was strange to me at first, but the longer I've been here, the more it just *fits* us. At this point, it's just the parties that we attend on a regular basis, but if that changes in the future, then I have no doubt we'll talk it through and find the best past forward for us—and any partners we engage with.

It's a...relief...to know that one person doesn't have to be my everything the way I was taught. I love Rusalka with everything I have. That doesn't change the way my heart flutters a little with Zhenya's hand in mine as ze leads me to where Danik and Feofan sit on a love seat, a glass of wine in each of their hands. "They're finally here!"

Danik smiles at me, flames dancing along his skin. "Inna only arrived a few minutes ago. They're hardly late."

"I'm impatient. Let me live." Zhenya wraps zir arms around my waist and props zir chin on my shoulder. I can feel Rusalka's gaze on us, and it makes me squirm in the best way possible. All of the succubi and incubi in the room notice it. How could they not when they can sense my desire? Zhenya presses a kiss to my cheek. "Gods, you all bring me so much joy."

I reach up with suddenly shaking hands, and I swear every person in the room focuses on me with a level of attention I can feel like a physical touch. I lift the birth control pendant—a gift from Azazel—from over my head and set it down carefully on the table next to Danik and Feofan's chair. "I'm ready."

No one responds with words, but magic charges through the room. When we discussed this party and how it would be different than past ones, Rusalka and I decided that we'd like to have the Insomnior Court be part of the process in a very real way. All except Zhenya agreed—ze said "Not me, love. I'm happy being bibi to all the little ones and not have any of my own." Ze is still here, of course. Zhenya loves a party more than most and wouldn't miss this for the world.

Feofan takes my hand and tugs me down to straddle him. "You look lovely tonight." He cups my hips as Danik shifts to stand behind me, replacing Zhenya. I catch sight of them drifting over to Rusalka, to sink between her spread thighs. Our gaze meets in a charged moment that makes me shiver.

This is happening.

If everything goes to plan, tonight I'll end up pregnant with a baby that's *ours*. Mine. Hers. The Insomnior Court's. The entire territory's. To be loved and cherished and raised with the option of being territory leader after Rusalka steps down. But only if they want to. They will be raised with an abundance of love that still baffles me on my bad days. They will *never* be taught to feel shame for something that is natural and hurts no one.

Danik skates his hand down my stomach to part my robe, and Feofan anticipates him, already stroking me between my legs. I don't need succubus or incubus magic to call the surge of desire I feel in response. It's all me. It's all *joy*.

I lose myself in their touch, in my touching them in turn. Pleasure ebbs and flows in a lazy seduction that only makes everything hotter. Especially when Danik's lips brush my ear and he says. "We'd like to take you together."

Together.

I shiver, already nodding. "Yes. Absolutely."

Feofan laughs softly. "We thought you might say that." He tugs me down until his cock presses to my entrance. "Relax, darling. We've got you."

Relax. An impossible task when I'm quivering with anticipation. We've done this before—Danik and Feofan, yes, but also Rusalka and Inna and other combinations. It's become one of my favorite things. I lean back against Danik as Feofan works me down his cock until we're sealed together. A blush works its way through his light-brown cheeks, his flames dancing higher around us. "Now Danik."

Neither of them have chosen to be particularly massive tonight, but there's *two* of them and the fit is tight enough to throw back my head. At least until I feel the very familiar sensation of Rusalka's attention on me. Of *their* flames reaching across the distance to stroke my face.

I open my eyes to find them watching me, their eyes heavy-lidded with pleasure as Zhenya licks their pussy while Inna fucks ze from behind, holding zir hair back so I can see clearly how ze works Rusalka with zir tongue. It makes me shiver, which in turn makes Danik and Feofan moan in pleasure.

They kiss over me even as they fuck me slowly, their cocks filling me almost to the point of pain. I can't move well in this position, so I give myself over to their movement, their touch. Building and building and building until I feel like I might die if I don't come.

Rusalka's flame cascades down my chest and over my stomach to press to my clit as Danik and Feofan pick up their pace. "Together," Danik mutters in a strained voice.

"Together," Feofan echoes, his grip spasming on my hips.

The pressure against my clit increases, pulsing in exactly the way I need. "Together," I gasp. It's as if the word unlocks my climax, shuddering through me as Danik and Feofan's pace increases and then they're coming too, filling me with their seed.

They barely ease out of me before Inna appears at our side. "My turn, love." They scoop me up and carry me to the couch where Rusalka reclines, Zhenya now in her lap, her hand between zir thighs. Inna topples me down next to them and presses my legs wide. They laugh, the sound pure seduction. "Feofan and Danik filled you right up, didn't they?"

I look down my body to where the evidence of that is all over my pussy and thighs. It makes my whole body clench. "Yes."

"Then you're ready for me." Tonight, their cock is bigger than normal with a wicked curve that I already know I'm going to enjoy immensely. They press me wide as they enter me in one slow stroke. I reach out without looking, catching Rusalka's free hand and lacing my fingers with hers as Inna fucks me. They pound into me, making my back bow and my eyes roll back in my head.

Inna kisses me as they come, filling me and then over-filling me. Seed gushes down my thighs as they pull back, grabbing Zhenya around the waist and lifting ze with them. "Come here, you."

Zhenya's joyful giggle makes me smile. I slump down next to Rusalka and watch Danik and Feofan make out, shifting against each other in a way that makes me think they're recovering from their orgasms faster than normal.

"Come here, little one." Rusalka tugs me up to straddle them and cups my face. "Are you ready?"

"For you? Always?"

They kiss me slowly as their flesh stirs between us, their form shifting to accommodate a penis. I've known they could do this for years, but it's one threshold we haven't crossed. Rusalka's always used their fire or fingers or tongue. But tonight is different in a lot of ways, so it stands to reason that it will be different in this way, too.

Their claws prick my ass as they lift me onto their cock, before those change too, morphing into fingers. I kiss them with everything I have, and then when that's not enough, I whisper, "I love you so much, Rusalka. I want to have a baby with you."

"After tonight, there's a decent chance you will." She eases me down her cock, going so slow that I have to resist the urge to rush her. Rusalka shifts one of her hands to the base of my neck. "But I'm selfish in that I hope you don't end up pregnant right away." She strokes my clit as she fucks up into me, one lazy stroke at a time. "I liked watching the others fill you, little one."

"I liked it...too." I can barely keep my eyes open. My earlier orgasms have nothing on the one that's coming, building on the pleasure that came before. "I'm close."

"I know," they say simply. "Take me, little one. Take every drop."

My orgasm reaches a crescendo and my body takes over, grinding down on their cock even as Rusalka curses under their breath and comes deep inside me. They shift, laying me down on the couch and kissing me thoroughly, but make no move to withdraw. "I love you, Belladonna. Beyond words."

I can barely open my eyes, but I wrap my arms and legs around her. "I love you, too. So much sometimes I think I can't breathe past it."

Rusalka's low chuckle makes me shiver. "Keep breathing, little one. We have hours before dawn and we intend to use every bit of them."

THANK you so much for reading Rusalka and Belladonna's story! If you enjoyed it, please consider leaving a review. Be sure you don't miss any news about Azazel and Eve's book by signing up for my newsletter!

ABOUT THE AUTHOR

Katee Robert (she/they) is a *New York Times* and USA Today bestselling author of spicy romance. *Entertainment Weekly* calls their writing "unspeakably hot." Their books have sold over two million copies. They live in the Pacific Northwest with their husband, children, a cat who thinks he's a dog, and two Great Danes who think they're lap dogs.

Website: www.kateerobert.com

Newsletter: https://dashboard.mailerlite.com/forms/228943/118255546612582170/share

facebook.com/AuthorKateeRobert

instagram.com/katee_robert

threads.net/@katee_robert

tiktok.com/@authorkateerobert

bookbub.com/profile/katee-robert

patreon.com/kateerobert

Made in the USA
Middletown, DE
11 November 2024

64342277R00109